D1224983

BLACK SWAN

A HUTCHINSON NOVELLA

General Editor: Frank Delaney

CHRISTOPHER HOPE
HOPE
•BLACK SWAN•

WITH ILLUSTRATIONS BY
GILLIAN BARLOW

HUTCHINSON

LONDON   MELBOURNE   AUCKLAND   JOHANNESBURG

General Editor: Frank Delaney

Series Design by Craig Dodd

© Christopher Hope 1987

Illustrations © Gillian Barlow 1987

Grateful acknowledgement is given for permission to quote from *Everybody's Autobiography* by Gertrude Stein, published by Virago Press, 1985

This edition first published in Great Britain in 1987
by Hutchinson, an imprint of Century Hutchinson Ltd,
Brookmount House, 62–65 Chandos Place, London WC2N 4NW

Century Hutchinson South Africa Pty Ltd.
PO Box 337, Bergvlei, 2012 South Africa

Century Hutchinson Australia (Pty) Ltd.
PO Box 496, 16–22 Church Street, Hawthorn, Victoria 3122, Australia

Century Hutchinson New Zealand Ltd.
PO Box 40-086, Glenfield, Auckland 10, New Zealand

British Library Cataloguing in Publication Data

Hope, Christopher
  Black swan.
  I. Title
  832 [F]   PR9369.3.H6/

ISBN 0 09 172542 9

Typeset in Monophoto Photina by
Vision Typesetting, Manchester

Printed in Great Britain by
Butler & Tanner Ltd, Frome and London

For Jasper

'Two things are always the same, the dance and war.'
Gertrude Stein

ONE

They called him 'Lucky'. It was said he had been named after the brand of cigarettes his father smoked – *Lucky Strike*. 'Strike' would have been better, it was suggested. This was a township joke. Some things did best when struck: drums, gongs, matches . . . and the boy, Lucky. As a result, he grew to become a swift runner. When he was older he had the occasional stone thrown at him. Or at least tossed in his direction, not with any particular malice but as someone will throw a stone into a lake in the hopes of stirring it up, or pitch a pebble into a deep well and listen for the distant splash. Lucky was so remote, disinterested, so determinedly elsewhere that he provoked this kind of reaction.

There was no one to verify the story of how he got his name. His father had departed long before Lucky was old enough to register an impression of the man. Yet he thought he remembered him because of the cigarettes. This was a popular brand in the township and he saw the blurred oblong pack in many shirt pockets, with its round red eye like a target over the heart. There were also several large posters erected on the outskirts of the township on the main road that led to the white city; these showed a gleaming man in a bush-hat smiling widely, a packet of cigarettes invitingly proffered in his strong fist, the knuckles of which shone like beads: *Give A Man A Lucky!* the poster said. Lucky could not read what it said, but he did not care. Secretly, he considered this man to be his father. He told no one because it was probably not allowed. This big man with his huge smile was almost certainly someone else's father, or the property of the government. He was important, strong, rich and healthy. He had the same tough good looks as the film stars

1

they idolized at the Bantu Men's Social Centre where Humphrey Bogart and James Cagney films played. Down in the small theatre, with its rackety projector presided over by the bitter Methodist Sam Mafekong, where the smart men congregated – guys like Sweetchild Tsetse, Little Lester and Two-Can Mafeti. The man on the cigarette poster looked down at Lucky as if to say, 'You're with me, kid . . .' But if the man got to hear that Lucky claimed him as a father he would surely repudiate it angrily – for how on earth could such a clean, handsome man be the father of a mad boy, cursed by an evil spirit?

That was what his Granny, Muriel, said. She had delivered this verdict after taking him to the clinic run by the Lutheran Church in the township. The German doctor there had told Muriel that Lucky was living in another world – that he was of another category.

'No. He is mad.' Muriel spoke with immense but weary authority. 'The doctor must say what this madness is and give medicine. I cannot pay,' she added quickly. 'I am poor. And I must look after this mad boy. Life is terrible. If God looks down on this boy, he must shake his head and think to himself: "Ai, ai, something had gone very wrong here. This boy is too *dom!* Stupid. Like a rock. But it cannot be I, God, who makes this mistake because I am God and cannot make mistakes." Therefore, at the moment of birth it happened that an evil spirit interfered with the boy, or even that this *tokoloshe* entered into this boy's mother . . . For this is what the *tokoloshe* likes, to enter women when they are not knowing what's what.'

The German doctor at the Lutheran Mission listened in polite silence. She was not unsympathetic, but she was tired. She was even perhaps a trifle disenchanted. She dreamed of forests deep and dark, of mushroom picking. Her many years in the township had been a stern test of Christian ideals – and western medicine. Perhaps the *tokoloshe* really did exist and should be taken seriously. People brawled, drank, killed without reason. The little troll or demon with its huge sensual energies and capacities for mischief was frequently invoked. The doctor came from Cologne and secretly she cherished thoughts of her imminent retirement. She hoped to find a little house, perhaps outside Freiburg. And drink good coffee again. She longed for green fields and forests everywhere, she desperately desired shade. The rolling plains of the
2 Highveld depressed her. There were few trees in the Transvaal and the

township was a giant, dusty, leafless place. Thousands of little houses of brick or concrete stretched away from the eye in every direction.

She knew she was expected to enter into a kind of bargaining with the fierce, withered woman before her. This was a challenge to her European medicine. She was expected to make claims for her own science against the powers of the witch-doctor, the *sangoma*. The challenge irked her. The doctor had dealt for many years with township diseases, with spindly legs, distended stomachs, cholera, glaucoma, kwashiorkor, with measles and mumps as well as with stabbings, burns and bullet wounds. She understood the necessity for making a show with foreign drugs and flamboyant measures. The *tokoloshe* and his like were powerful. White medicine was war. In her time in the township she had enjoyed a reasonable success rate and the Lutheran Clinic was trusted by its patients. But many of them retained an equal degree of trust in the witch-doctor, the *sangoma*, or the healer, called the *ngaka*. So she found it irritating to be challenged to a duel, particularly over a boy whom no medicine would cure.

'Your grandson is not really sick. Just slow.' The doctor tapped her forehead. 'He is sleepy in the head.'

'Then we must wake him up,' said Muriel firmly.

Firmness was her abiding characteristic. It had enabled her to work thirty years as a domestic servant, cooking, cleaning, ironing, child-minding for a succession of half a dozen white housewives in the big city. It had given her the strength to outlast three husbands, as well as to bury four babies – to buy their burial plots, sew their graveclothes and erect handsome stones in the hot red sand of the big windy cemetery on the ridge above the township. Graves which she attended regularly, polishing the grey marble headstones and raking little bits of shale and flint that littered the small plots.

There was one occasion when she enlisted the help of the boy Lucky in this religious duty at the time when his school had refused to keep him on. She thought that the activity would be good for him. Lucky had seemed to enjoy it, swabbing the marble headstones with water from the bucket and then breathing on them as if he were polishing windows and grinning delightedly at his faint, ghostly reflection. He took particular joy in polishing the golden letters of the name of Muriel's children: Ruth, Sarah, Caleb, Rachel. Each stone carried the name, date

3

of death and the simple words 'Your Mother'. Lucky licked his fingertip and traced the names while Muriel hacked at the tough yellow grass, often taller than she was, which continually encroached on the graves.

Muriel was touched by his concern; this sort of work might conceivably benefit him. So it was that on one occasion she had allowed Lucky to go on his own to the graveyard. When he failed to return by mid-afternoon she went in search and found him asleep in the shade of a headstone. It was not surprising that he was tired – he had been busy. Each of the graves was covered with an elaborate pattern of stones: fine white flints for Ruth, round brown pebbles for Caleb, slender flakes of shale fitted like jigsaw pieces for Sarah and Rachel. Intricate designs of circles, squares and diagonals which must have taken him most of the day – and doubtless accounted for his exhaustion – decorated the little plots where her babies lay. In her rage and alarm, Muriel beat Lucky awake and then raked the graves clear of their strange adornments while the boy gazed on in anguish. Of course, after that she did not dare allow him near the graves again. Who knew what he might do the next time?

Muriel had also brought up her four children who had survived, seen them through school and into good jobs. Now she looked after the children of her children.

'To wake up this boy will take time,' said the doctor.

Muriel's look softened. 'He is the son of a cousin of my brother's wife who is a bad girl. She met a man from the gold mines. You know the old story. He never came no more afterwards. He promised to send money, but he never came. Now this girl, she works there by the other side of the city in a dress shop. She goes clackety-clack on her heels. Pink lips like fire!' Muriel swayed on imaginary stiletto heels and swung her buttocks. She pursed her lips and pretended to apply lipstick – then with the wave of a hand she dismissed with contemptuous scorn Lucky's frivolous absentee mother. 'She don't want Lucky. What can Lucky do in the city? He is mad. That's what this girl says. This girl says so about her own son!'

The doctor looked at the boy. Lucky averted his eyes. He was very thin. She reckoned his age as being somewhere between fifteen and seventeen. He wore a pair of filthy khaki shorts and a white sweat-shirt advertising a yo-yo competition organized by Coca-Cola. His eyes were

4

huge and dark, cheekbones high and prominent. The muscles of the calves, thighs and neck stood out stiffly and were well developed. But then Lucky spent much time running. He was never still. Even when he stood in one place, some part of him was bending, flexing, tensing. He placed one bare foot on top of the other and entwined his toes, swivelled his head and stared at the roof. He opened his mouth and tapped his front tooth, an aid he often employed when he 'went away'.

Beneath the scrutiny of the doctor from Cologne, Lucky was preparing to go away now. When he went away he left his body and entered his mind, which took off like a bird or a plane for somewhere else. It might be a land across the sea where giants played with tigers and feasted upon roasted sheep. It might be a secret cave in the mountains where he would live utterly unknown to the world, feeding upon prickly pears and drinking water caught in leaves, his only friends the jackals and baboons. Oh yes, Lucky could go anywhere. The place might be wild or pretty, he didn't really mind. Its great attraction was that it took him away from where he was. Lucky told no one of this ability to escape. He felt sure it was not allowed. No doubt there were ways of preventing him from leaving on these flights. Worse still, there were sure to be ways of bringing him back.

He also had ways of defending himself. He had only to look hard at an enemy and he disappeared. Or he could change them into anything he liked. Telephone poles. Or dogs. He called this 'doing away' with people. It was a power he had mentioned to his Granny Muriel, but she had begged him never to use it.

The doctor saw before her a teenage boy indistinguishable from a thousand other waifs, strays and urchins who constituted the rich undergrowth of the township. Some were in school, many were not. A few were determined to succeed. Most were tough, sharp, excitable, living on scraps, on white bread and Coke, on what they could beg or steal. Those children who went to school were at least manageable for a time. But after school and at night they roamed the township, drifting through the dusty streets like leaves blown by the wind, like spies, or stray dogs or beggars – laughing, stealing, yelling, longing to be big. Big like the bigger boys who dressed in tight black or white trousers with shiny jackets and who hung out of the windows of taxis and whistled at girls. These same bigger boys formed gangs and fought each other.

Some mornings bodies stuffed the doorways of the township's pleasure resorts, the back alleys where the shebeens were located, the shabby fleshpots which, as they said, only looked good when the lights were out. Blood ran in the dust. The young thugs also hung out on pay-day at the bus terminus and rail stations, any place where the crowds returned bringing their weekly wages earned in the white city, fat pickings for the tough boys with their knives and coshes, their flat cold eyes and the sort of cool mincing style learnt from the American gangster movies so beloved every Saturday night at the Bantu Men's Social Centre over the road from Peejay Stores, on 31st Street. They watched films about Mad Dog Coll, Pretty Boy Floyd and Lucky Luciano, which provided them with style, sent them crazy for big Pontiacs and Lincoln Continentals, gave them clumsy American accents and gang names like the New York Mohawks and the Zoot Boys. When the gangsters in these movies shot a cop the audience cheered. When a hoodlum fell they booed and threw ice-creams at the screen. The names of the local heroes were many, various, vivid: Chop-Chop Molefe and Big Boy Mantanzima, the Duke and Mr Ice. And all dreamed of becoming Public Enemy Number One. To the boys who wished to be like them, they seemed very tall, smart and utterly wonderful. Lucky gazed up at them with fear and wonderment, feeling a faint loosening in the bowels.

'Can he speak?'

'Speak to the doctor,' Muriel instructed.

'Hello,' said Lucky.

'You see, he speaks well,' said Muriel.

'Hello, hello, hello – do you receive me? – over . . .' said Lucky.

'He thinks he is a wireless,' said Muriel and shook her head. 'He is always thinking he is something. But he isn't. He is just sick. He speaks well, but he has got nothing to say.'

'And today, a story of adult love and passion. We bring you Dr Paul . . .' Lucky pronounced in a deep voice with a warm American accent.

'Hello, Lucky,' the doctor repeated helplessly.

'Do you listen to the radio? Then you will know this programme. Love and passion,' Muriel said with scorn. 'For a boy! What kind of boy is that? This boy cannot read or write. But he sings everything on the radio. And speaks in voices. But does he understand? Not nothing! Look here.' She seized Lucky's shoulder and shook him. 'Look, look! See his eyes. He is going somewhere. Lucky, stay! He is always going somewhere, this boy, when you want him.'

'You mean he runs away?'

Muriel shrieked, 'Runs away! That will be the frosty Friday. He goes away in his body, nowhere . . . but in his head, ai! ai! he is never here. Always somewhere else. He is driving me crazy!'

The doctor examined Lucky. She looked into his ears, his mouth, his eyes. She tested his reflexes.

'This is what I suggest to you, Muriel. We are starting a school here out in the clinic. A special school, for people like Lucky. You can bring him here and we will try to help him. But it will take time.'

'I have not time,' snapped Muriel. 'I need medicine. Now! Come, Lucky.' She shook him roughly. 'We are going to the *sangoma,* she will give us medicine.'

The doctor sighed. 'We will keep a place for him. If you change your mind, bring him back. Goodbye, Lucky.'

But Lucky didn't hear her. His eyes were glazed. He had already left.

Lucky had gone kite-flying. This had become a favourite occupation ever since the Chinese boy had shown him how to make a kite. The Chinese boy accompanied his father, the Fahfee man, who came each week to the township in his cream Oldsmobile to collect the takings. The arrival of the Fahfee man was a big day. The wealth of the Chinaman was clear in the fact that here was a man who brought with him his own shade. There was very little shade in the township and none in the dusty square where the Chinaman parked his Oldsmobile. But simply by opening the great door of the car, a fat red rich leather wing, the little Chinese boy made himself an island of shade where he sat on the ground and built his kite.

First he took two thin pieces of cane and lashed them into a cross, using pink cotton thread to bind them. He cut notches at the ends of the pieces of bamboo and strung the pink cotton round the frame. Then he fetched from the glove compartment of his father's car a roll of thin green paper. What paper that was! Was there ever such a green? It was

7

the colour of grass in picture books of England. It was sweet and frozen, the colour of tubular ices on sticks which the ice-cream man sold from his cart when he came pedalling by on his bike, ringing his plump silver bell, and all the township children heard his piercing whistle that sounded both sharp and rusty at the same time. It was the green of the neon cross on the roof of the Adventist Church on 16th Avenue. A green to sniff, touch and to eat was the green of the kite paper the little Chinese boy snipped with his scissors in the shade of his father's huge Oldsmobile, with its red leather seats and an assortment of small imitation shrunken heads dangling from the driving mirror.

The Chinaman was not often in the township. Usually he worked the rich suburbs in the white city some miles away where the black domestic servants flocked to play. People bet on their dreams and that was how Fahfee worked. The Chinaman and his assistant were checking their bags of money. There was a good deal of it and it was unlikely that the Chinaman would have allowed these operations to be observed had he not known that the tall thin lad with the dreamy eyes who stood watching, tugging at his lower lip and twining the bare toes of one foot in the other, was harmless. They paid no more attention to him than they did to the small rooster which also wandered over to watch the proceedings in the dusty square. The Fahfee man wore dark glasses and his thin dark hair was plastered with oil. His black assistant, who was also his driver and bodyguard, held the bags while the Chinaman counted the contents, spreading the money out on the back seat, and began sending the beads of the abacus skidding along the wire frame. It was very quiet, the only sounds the click of the beads, the Chinese boy's noisy breathing as he concentrated on his kite-making and the occasional dry peck as the rooster's beak investigated some passing morsel. The money on the back seat represented the bets laid by people who backed their dreams. The runners who worked for the Fahfee man would have collected these bets and handed them to the pullmen, who in turn handed them over to the Chinaman when he came cruising by in his big Oldsmobile. He would not stop, but merely slowed down and handed to the pullman a scrap of paper on which the winning number was written. The pullman then signalled to the lucky winners the special number that took the prize. The signs to indicate the number were known to all. Hiking up an imaginary skirt meant a

prostitute; there were also the cow, the pig, the white woman, the tiger and many others. Today the pullman had made the sign for the teacher. He had drawn a finger around his collar, a gesture that looked as if he were cutting his throat. Those watching knew then that thirty was the lucky number.

The Chinese boy laid the skeleton of his kite upon the edible green paper and fetched from inside the car a pot of glue. Lucky's salivary glands once more began to over-react. The glue was mixed from flour and water and made him hungry. Now, with his finger, the boy primed the edges of the paper and then wrapped them over the cotton rigging. There! The cool, green, skinny diamond shivered and rustled as the Chinese boy held it in the air and tested his creation. The Chinese boy blew through his lips the sound of the wind. 'Wooh, wooh!' Lucky licked his lips and his stomach growled softly. The kite was the most beautiful thing he had ever seen. The rooster pecked at a small steel button – fallen from some man's jeans, perhaps – which lay in the red dust.

The money was now all counted and the engine growled. The Chinese boy and kite disappeared into the hot, peppery leathery interior of the car which sped away, spitting dust and pebbles. Having checked the takings of his runners against the tallies, the Chinaman was on his way to pay off the happy winner who had dreamed of teachers and laid his bet on number thirty. The rooster turned a bright angry eye on the disappearing limousine and then delicately ate the button.

Lucky did not look after the car. He barely registered its departure. He was far too busy recalling the steps needed to build a kite. He shook with delight at the gift which the Chinese boy had so generously given him.

He had built many kites since that day. He was building a kite now as he walked with Granny Muriel to consult the herbalist, the *ngaka*, whose name was Marigold. The herbalist was a friend of Muriel's, a woman with a large beaked nose and a fleshy smile. They sat in her dark, sweltering room beneath portraits of Queen Elizabeth II and Chief Albert Luthuli. Marigold the *ngaka* was cheaper than the witch-doctor. She threw the bones; four elephant ivory bones and four small seashells. They scattered on her table which was covered with linoleum in black and white diamonds, the shape of kites. The look of the table entranced Lucky. It seemed to him like the ceiling of a fairy palace or the

brain of a magician, where everything altered yet where everything was exact, balanced, the black and white rectangles dancing on their points.

'See how his eyes widen,' Marigold whispered. 'The bones say there is a journey he will take. Soon, maybe.'

Muriel nodded in satisfaction. 'He may soon travel to a new school in the Lutheran Mission. The doctor there says he must come . . . if other people cannot help him.'

Marigold pondered the implication of this. 'The boy is hurt by the *tokoloshe*.'

Muriel nodded with satisfaction at this well-judged reply. 'It is true. His mother was probably entered by the *tokoloshe*. She is a bad girl. Her boy is like a bird. He flies everywhere, but his home is nowhere.' Muriel fluttered her arms in exasperation.

Marigold stood up – round, polished and gleaming. Her green and gold dress rustled about her. 'I will show him the wall.'

'Yes, the wall may be good,' Muriel agreed. 'How much?'

'Five shillings.'

It was not cheap. On the other hand she would undoubtedly have to pay something to the clinic for Lucky's food if he went there. It seemed to Muriel worth the investment. The wall treatment had been impressive in other cases.

'Yes. Show him the wall,' she said.

Muriel drew the curtains in the small hot room and brown, wet warmth fell on them. They could hear the iron roof above them ticking in the heat. Muriel switched on a small cycle lamp which she trained on a blank white wall behind her. Then she put her hand on Lucky's shoulder. 'What do you see? Tell us what you see on the wall.'

'The moon,' replied Lucky promptly. 'It is round like the belly of a white woman who is carrying a child.'

'What else?' Marigold prompted.

'On the moon live seven black giants.'

Muriel whispered loudly, 'What does this mean?'

Marigold touched her finger to her temples and covered her eyes. She was clearly unsure of what to make of this flowing exoticism.

'And the spears of these black giants are made of gold,' Lucky continued memorably, 'and they ride to battle on the mountains as if on the backs of bulls.'

Muriel challenged the prophetess. 'What is this? Bulls and giants?' *11*

Marigold opened her eyes, looking puzzled and embarrassed. 'It is difficult. When people look at the wall they usually see spirits . . . of their ancestors. Or pictures of money. Or snakes. These things I know and I say what they mean. They mean that money comes. Or you must visit your parents. Or take a special medicine. Okay, this is usual. But never the moon with giants!'

Muriel rose to her feet. 'This boy can find the sun in a glass of water!' she cried. 'He can take your wall and break it like an egg – and every piece of the wall will grow inside his head into elephants and gangsters and queens of England. This is true! I know this. So I come to ask you what to do. I am waiting to hear you, my sister.' A dangerous note had entered Muriel's voice.

Marigold heard it. 'Some I cannot diagnose. For some I must dance so that the spirit is moved to tell me what it is we must do with this boy who dreams of giants and bulls.'

Without further delay, Marigold began to dance. She stamped one foot then the other, at the time clicking her fingers in a complicated rhythm while crooning a long, sweet note. Lucky found it satisfying. He especially liked the way Marigold made the note shiver upwards so that he thought it must break its head against the roof, and then pulled it back safely into her throat. Muriel, however, was not impressed. This dance she had seen before; it was performed every Sunday in the Mine Compound by young men from the Venda tribe. The young men wore green shirts, white trousers and sandshoes on which so much whitewash had been lavished that they glowed with a brilliant beauty which snatched at the heart. The dance was better performed by the lithe young men in the green shirts – and, moreover, it cost nothing. Marigold, on the other hand, was charging five shillings for this performance and might even, given the difficulty of the case, decide to increase the price.

Muriel fished in her rubbery black leather purse which she kept on a leather strap that hung about her neck, and found two half-crowns. It was enough, yes. She would give Lucky to the Germans. She did not blame Marigold for being unable to offer an effective treatment, recognising better than anybody that he was probably untreatable. She looked at the boy who sat enraptured by the dance. The two half-crowns in Muriel's fingers were warm, for she kept her rubbery purse dangling between her breasts where it was safe. Lucky's mouth was open and his eyes white and bright. She knew that look. He was doing things with the prophetess. It was not right. You should not do as you liked with other people the way Lucky did. Nor should you fly away in your head whenever you felt like it. Muriel feared for the boy in the township. Some day someone would get angry with him.

Lucky felt none of her concern. He was watching Marigold greedily. He saw her in the sky, floating heavily in her green clothes, a dark storm cloud full of rain that drifts over fields of young maize – round, fat and full of promise.

TWO

It took all her training and self-discipline not to hit Lucky within a week of knowing him. She, who recoiled from violence and who never dreamed she would ever feel anger, would never have any part to play in the old, dirty business of pushing people around when she came to work in Africa. She came from Stuttgart and was trained to work with what were called 'educationally sub-normal children'. Her name was Ilse and she looked younger than her twenty-one years, perhaps because she wore her blonde hair almost as short as a boy's and her forehead was broad and bold – creased by a small and rather pretty frown which grew deeper and less appealing during her early weeks at the Lutheran Mission in the township. She knew nothing of Africa except that it needed trained nurses and teachers. She looked at South Africa in the atlas and found it brown and empty. She was told that relations between the races were not good, that whites and blacks were separated. She imagined them as living in parallel camps. But the Lutheran Mission was permitted in the black township because it was a charity. And the staff were foreigners. The doctor from Cologne took Ilse under her wing, and gave her a piece of advice: the politics of the country were strange and deeply confusing. Nothing was as it seemed. Besides, those for whom she would be caring were so disadvantaged they never entered the political arena.

Of course there was in any event a good deal to trouble and confuse her. There was Africa itself. She arrived in July, flying out of the heat of Europe, and found herself shivering on the Highveld two thousand metres above sea-level. The thin air and the faint blue sky soaring overhead made her dizzy. She kept on shaking her head as if some extraordinary piece of knowledge secretly troubled her, or as if to remind herself that at last she really was out of Germany and somewhere else. The days were bright and blue, with an edge to them that cut across the unprotected neck or ear which, only a moment before, the sun had been warming pleasantly. The nights were dark, clear, icily crystal. The grass was yellow and powdery, burnt by the night chill and the high dry heat of the glittering winter days. The sky was a polished pond which rebuffed the eye. It sent her glance skipping across its surface like a stone over still water. The distance to the horizon oppressed and frightened her. The bleak blue sky looked hard as metal, arching in a great curve to meet the veld far in the distance. This was a high, dry, indifferent landscape which dwarfed the township and shrunk it to a scattering of tiny houses and tin shacks, a scurf of development, an eruption upon the otherwise iron red veld. And yet the township was enormous, she knew that. It contained two to three times as many people as the white city fifteen kilometres away, with its skyscrapers and motorways. Yet it seemed smaller, less significant, impermanent.

At first she imagined, coming from Stuttgart, that the township had been built to remain impermanent. Surely no one seriously expected to live for very long in these little brick houses? They looked to her not much bigger than the garage at home which housed her father's DKW. In fact, as she soon discovered, the houses were certainly regarded by the people who lived in them as being permanent. The occupants, at least, felt them to have been built to last for ever. And often numbered five or six or seven, with still more people –friends, relations or tenants – housed in sheds, lean-tos and clumsy extensions at the backs of the houses. Yet these dwellings seemed to her bare, small, unforgiving and ugly. They had neither electric light nor piped water nor sewage facilities. For these were the 1960s and to someone from Stuttgart, this backwater came as a great shock. She did not understand how people found the determination to grow large beds of dahlias – colossal things with the heads of mad poodles pushing through the fences at the fronts of the houses – or to polish the red steps until they gleamed with the colour of newly-spilt blood, or why they buffed the old brass stand-taps that supplied water to the street until they shone a grainy gold. She

15

never got used to any of this. Nor to the smoke from thousands of coal fires which banked heavy and grey overhead each evening. Nor to the children wearing nothing but a shirt, running about showing their bare buttocks. Nor to the stink of sewage, the drunks rolling home from the beer halls or the smart young men with the menacing airs who wore the cheapest, most horribly loud American clothes and hung about the dusty bus-stops as if parading outside some favourite hoodlums' bar in deepest Chicago. Nor even to the light which drew a knife across the eyes at unexpected moments, nor to the taste of the red township dust that seemed always on her tongue.

The Lutheran Mission, she came to recognise, was in the better part of town. You passed the police training ground, turned left at the back of the Anglican church, drove downhill, passed the artificial lake where the empty milk bottles floated among the lilies, passed the Central Trading Store, the sports arena and the funeral parlour and arrived at the Lutheran Mission beside St Mary's Crèche for the children of working mothers. The Mission was in fact a group of bungalows with extensive grounds. A large room at the rear of the house was given over to the new school for the mentally disadvantaged. The children who came to the new teacher from Stuttgart in those first days ranged from a boy in his early twenties called Seraphim to a tiny little girl named China, who kept her eyes closed all the time.

There were six pupils in all, the numbers going up or down for a variety of reasons during the weeks that followed. The doctor from Cologne examined them all and offered diagnoses of their conditions. None was particularly hopeful. The big boy, Seraphim, was autistic and little progress could be expected. Several of the other children were schizophrenic and might possibly respond to treatment, The little girl called China had been so badly traumatised by her drunken father, who had beaten her and burnt her with cigarette ends, that she would perhaps respond best over a period of months not to any formal approaches but simply to a warm maternal presence.

'But I think you're probably going to find the boy Lucky is the most difficult. He's hyperactive. Intelligent, of course, yet he proves impossible to communicate with. He's in another world. Another category altogether. Of course I'm not saying you won't win, we all win if we try hard enough. And long enough!' The doctor from Cologne laughed ruefully. 'Maybe something will work if you can find a way of seizing on that energy of his. Try to direct it. Push it towards some goal. Maybe that way you'll get him to respond, to react to the world as it is, not as he sees it in his head.'

The doctor from Cologne had used the word 'category' to refer to Lucky. It was a word towards which Ilse felt a special antipathy; a word familiar, she believed, to older Germans especially. Ilse was very sensitive about the use of the word. Her parents and teachers called her over-sensitive. Certainly it got her off to an unfortunate start with the doctor and an even worse beginning with the boy Lucky.

But then she was not to know. To be trained to go out to fulfil what you believe to be your mission in life, to start off feeling confident, bold and happy and then to find within hours, even minutes of your arrival at your destination that there is something in the air you do not understand – this would trouble even a less sensitive person.

As a small girl this trembling awareness of forces and currents in the air had given Ilse a particular grace and delicacy in the ballet lessons she took three times a week. She had wanted desperately to be a dancer. But that was long ago . . . long before she had first heard the word 'category'. She had heard her father use it in connection with the Nuremberg Laws passed by the National Socialists in 1935. Those laws, her father explained one day for no particular reason, were certainly not an attempt to discriminate against the Jews. On the contrary, just as the government of the time had recognised the right of Jews to give all their loyalty to their faith, so also there were those who believed that it was the right of true Germans to bind themselves to *their* nation with the same degree of freedom. After all – where was the harm? All the Nuremberg Laws had done, Ilse's father insisted, was to recognise that there was a German and a non-German category.

This had come as news to Ilse. At school her history contained the barest mention of the Nuremberg Laws. Indeed, when she tried to enquire further she found that examination of the war was not encouraged and the study of its reasons and beginnings was not on the school syllabus. Even so, she might never have taken the matter any further had her father not added with some anger, 'So now you know about different categories. What's so wrong with that? Different people in different categories?'

She remembered this distinctly. He had spoken these words after draining his small glass of kirsch with which he usually accompanied his cup of coffee in the evening and then he had delicately plucked from the glass the maraschino cherry which floated in the liqueur and eaten it with tiny nibbles, surprisingly feminine in a man who was large, stocky and had served his country throughout the war 'in action so dangerous I dare not recall it even now . . .'

But who were the people who said the Nuremberg Laws were wrong? And why did they say so? These were questions that sent Ilse to the local library from which she returned sweating, nauseous and unable to sleep for several nights without dreaming such things that she cried out and wet her bed to her shame and misery, for she was then already fifteen. Nevertheless, she persisted in her reading and to her relief, after a time, the dreams grew less frequent and the bed-wetting did not recur, though she would return from the library white-faced and breathless and filled with an obscure, terrible sense of panic. The books she read obsessed her. The more she read, the more mystified she became. She stared at people passing in the street, trying to imagine them meeting the trucks which brought the prisoners to the camps, and ordering the gas. She tried to imagine her father taking a baby and smashing its skull against the steel sides of a railway car. She tried *hard*. But she could not do it. It was impossible.

But there it was. Now that she had started, she could not stop. There was so much to read. She began to begrudge the amount of time she had to give to her lessons. She cut her friends, took no interest in parties. At last – and not without a considerable struggle – she even gave up her ballet. It saved time and time was essential. Also these other activities seemed inappropriate in the light of what she knew. Her secret readings in German history continued and intensified. She attempted to raise the subject at school, but was rebuffed. After all, she was told, these were the 1960s and the war was long over. She was a child of a new Germany; it was unhelpful to dwell on past mistakes. Certainly, it seemed to her that her schoolmates were happily part of the new Germany. They did not wake at night. They grew their hair long, they experimented with hallucinogenic drugs and they talked of love, peace and flowers, they dreamt of leaving home to live in communes and spent large sums of money supporting the record industry.

She had a boyfriend called Boris, who was at trade school learning to be a joiner. He made the most exquisite wooden barrels with polished staves and copper hoops, and he touched the legs of tables as if they were living flesh. Boris was small and freckled and unhappy about his future career. He wore velvet doublets and his hair swept his shoulder-blades. The fact was that he wanted to become a pop star. He sang the latest hits from England and America quite faultlessly, though he understood no English at all, and the lyrics frequently made him weep. It was his gentleness which made Ilse fall in love with him. And the fact that her father hated his flowery, dreamy ways. For this reason too she allowed him to make love to her every Friday night after classes, usually after he had strummed through several of the latest ballads on his guitar. As her reading grew more intense and the information it revealed more terrible, she one night mentioned her secret to him. But Boris responded by saying that the spirit of the universe pulsed with love and peace. After which he sang to her about divinity in San Francisco and she knew that this was no answer. Soon Boris went the way of her ballet lessons and so much else.

Ilse found that there was nothing she could do with the knowledge gained from her trips to the library. But it grew inside her, bigger and bigger. It hid her from her friends, cut her off from her parents. Worst of all, it divided her from the happy child she had once been. Her walks to the library seemed to add to the distance growing between herself and her parents. Eventually she took to praying at the little Lutheran Church at the end of the road, where she paused each day to gather strength before facing her mother and father. She grew thin and pale. She wore no make-up and her blonde hair was scraped back and held in the plainest of brown rubber bands. Her mother and father were distressed; a pretty girl who did not dance, seldom smiled, took no interest in boys and went to church daily, seemed a very queer creature.

One day, in response to some glancing reference to the old Germany and in an attempt to alert them to her huge, heavy, yet uncommunicable knowledge of the German-Jewish disaster, she challenged the morality of the Nuremberg Laws in a long delayed answer to her father's demand to know what was wrong with the notion of different categories of people.

'Because it has killed people. The people in the wrong category,' Ilse suddenly said.

Her father looked perplexed, then weary, then suddenly angry. He understood.

'Look . . . In the world today, others have laws like this. Religious laws. About who can marry and who cannot. The Israelis do it themselves. Nobody complains. All we asked was the same for Germans.'

'Germany was threatened,' her mother added, 'encircled. Her enemies wished to destroy her. What could we do? We did not want war with England or America. We only wished to preserve our nation. We had to fight.'

'And would fight again,' her father insisted.

'Life is not all love and flowers the way they talk about it in your pop songs today,' her mother said.

'I hate those songs,' said Ilse with a vehemence which took her parents aback. They had never known her to hate anything.

A few weeks later she came across a photograph in the local paper which showed a group of men with their hats pulled down over their eyes congregated about the entrance to an hotel. According to the newspaper, these men were attending a secret SS reunion dinner in a town nearby. Among those slipping stealthily into the hotel she instantly recognised her father.

Ilse stopped going to school. Dropping out was increasingly fashionable. Many of her friends went to live in squats where they lit joss-sticks and listened to Indian ragas on elaborate stereophonic equipment, seeking a life uncorrupted by western materialism and feeling closer to the source of love and peace. Ilse's dropping-out, however, caused a scandal, for she applied to the Lutheran Church to train as a missionary. The course being residential, she went away. She never returned home. She specialised in dealing with what were known as 'disturbed children'. When she qualified she was posted to Africa together with her diploma, three pounds of German coffee for the doctor of the Lutheran Mission in the Southern African township, and an aching desire to stand between the innocent and the insane. Her English was scanty but adequate, her enthusiasm was enormous. She felt she could take on the world. She felt free at last.

The children sat in desks donated by the local German Club, which enthusiastically supported the special school. The desk-lids were seamed by old knife grooves, stained by the inks of generations and still smelt faintly of paper, bread, wax polish and oranges – traces of their previous lives in a primary school for white children. The desks gave an air of normality to the room. A black woman was appointed to help Ilse take care of the more difficult children. She would be glad of an extra pair of hands, the doctor explained to her.

Ilse stared. 'I do not wish a servant.'

The doctor said nothing; she merely raised her eyebrows. The black helper was withdrawn.

There was a small green writing board on a tripod, a few shelves of books, a stationery cupboard in the corner against the plain white-washed wall, several boxes of chalks and a board duster. Ilse pinned up a nature study chart showing birds, frogs and trees. She also hung up a map of the world and a calendar showing the Black Forest in all its seasons, a gift from the doctor. She arranged bunches of red and blue flowers which grew wild by the stand-pipe outside in the garden, to be displayed in vases. What they were called, these tough luxuriant blooms that flourished in winter, she neither knew nor cared. She was happy; she prepared to meet the life for which she had prayed and planned. The sense of order she established in her classroom, as she prepared to receive her pupils, was a way of asserting herself. By organizing the room to operate smoothly, she felt she was establishing some kind of defence against the wide blue vacancy she had found in the Africa outside the walls.

There were just six of them to start. She waited, eager, trained, willing and rather regretting the fact that they were so few in number – hardly sufficient to challenge her reserves of determination, patience and love. She confronted her own slight pangs of disappointment. Still, she told herself, six was only a start. When the programme got off the ground, others would follow. In her eagerness to establish a friendly atmosphere, she invited the children to sit wherever they chose and this led to immediate confusion. The three schizophrenics began fighting over the same desk, kicking and scratching each other; she was forced to intervene and allocate desks to them where they sat, stony-faced and breathing noisily. The big autistic boy, Seraphim, proved to be incontinent and left pools around the classroom. Little China sat in the front desk with her eyes tightly shut. Only Lucky seemed relaxed. True, there was a dreamy, rather vacant look in his eyes, but he seemed friendly and she immediately settled on him as the spokesman for the group.

Very quickly she recognized her mistake. This was no group and Lucky spoke, most alarmingly and vocally, only for himself. The curious thin, funny boy in his khaki shorts and his white teeshirt and the eyes that roamed about the room – darting into the corners and back again to her face – with an amused and yet somehow distant smile, had not one voice but any number. There was the exaggerated cowboy twang. There was a deep rich, sincere, adult voice, taken – as she soon discovered – from the radio soap operas starring Dr Paul: 'A Tale of Adult Love and Passion . . .' and there was infrequently, amidst snatches from pop shows and advertising jingles which he seemed to have playing inside his head most of the day, Lucky's own voice, surprisingly light and high in a boy whose age, on closer inspection, she estimated to be in the late teens. The radio shows from which he took these voices, as she was also to discover, were energetic, vulgar and plentiful and Lucky's gift for mimicry was quite extraordinarily developed.

For his part, Lucky took to Ilse immediately. 'I hope you'll be very happy amongst us, my dear,' he told her in his rich brown, Dr Paul voice.

When the children in the middle of the room began fighting and drew blood he saw how Ilse stood there paralysed with fear and pity and so he decided to explain to her how things were. He retained his medical voice for the occasion. 'These boys and girls, they're poor fish, my dear. They're frightened. They would be much happier somewhere else.'

'But why?' she wanted desperately to know. 'I am here to do all I can for them.'

'Because, dear heart,' Lucky intoned, 'these kids think that this is a prison and you are the jailer. Otherwise why bring them to this room? This special place? Answer me that. If this place be not a place of correction and grief?'

'Tell them I am their friend,' she said.

Lucky looked at her as if she were mad. At the same time he was conscious of a certain pang of disappointment. He was not interested in friends. What he wanted to know was – what could she give him? What could she tell him? Something perhaps about giants, genies, cowboys, gangsters? When he first heard her thick foreign accent, his heart had leapt. She was from overseas! She came from the world! He had looked particularly closely at her feet. They were small, dainty and clad in flat white shoes. Foreign shoes, made overseas. He longed to take those shoes and examine them more carefully for signs of their exotic origins. And those feet? They were surely worthy of examination too. Had they not walked on strange soil in the world over the sea? Ilse was from Stuttgart. He repeated the name. How musical! She was also the first being from another world with whom he had been friendly. He longed to walk up and touch her. And she came not just from another place but a better one – in short, she was from the world to come. There were other Germans in the Mission, but they had been there so long they were just like other ordinary white people, not magical beings from overseas.

For Lucky, overseas was the promised land. Of course he went there often and he had elaborated a variety of signs and associations which told him exactly where he had landed. Without maps, after all, a boy needed to know where he was. He drew his destinations from comics, magazines, picture books and, of course, the radio. When he went to America, for example, he recognised it by its sidewalk. It was a sidewalk on a hot Saturday afternoon, and there on the sidewalk a couple of kids were selling home-made lemonade from a pitcher which stood on a small table beside two or three glass tumblers. Behind the young vendors of lemonade were the outlines of skyscrapers. Naturally, Lucky knew there were other things in America. There were cowboys and crooks and Mickey Mouse. There were amusement parks. Yet these things were not real. But the hot afternoon, the sidewalk and the lemonade sellers – they were true. Just as true were the pink people of England who spoke in voices as grey and as green as the rain and the fog. It was through the grey, green fog that he plunged – down, down, down! – when he took one of his trips to England, plummeting out of the sky like Superman to land beside the soldier in the busby right outside Buckingham Palace. Of Germany, however, Lucky had no images. It was a place he had never thought of visiting. The women at the Lutheran Mission provided no inspiration. But now there was Ilse. She would be his Germany, with her fair hair, her pretty feet and her foreign accent. She spoke as if her tongue were wearing her shoe. She would be his Germany and he would know the country through her. He hoped it would be an interesting experience; he hoped she would co-operate. He did not wish to write her off, as he had had to write off so many in the past.

And yet Lucky was not interested in being friends. He watched Seraphim, who was sitting very still in his seat. Every so often Seraphim groaned. Lucky knew Seraphim well. Everyone did. For years the mad tall boy had wandered around the township relieving himself wherever he wished, squatting by the roadside quite openly so that the women passing gave expressions of dismay and disgust when they saw his bare backside. But they all knew he was soft in the head and they knew he meant no harm. Yet it had been a mistake to bring him into this room. Seraphim did not understand rooms. They had dressed him in a khaki shirt and shorts and a pair of sandals. That also was a mistake. Seraphim had never worn more than a shirt. Despite his name, he was not a pretty boy; he had a long thin jaw and large ears. Yet people were not ill-disposed towards him. They did not laugh at him in the way they laughed at Lucky. But there was something reckless about Lucky, something 'flighty' and they did not like that.

As Lucky watched Seraphim he was conscious of a smell, heavy and rank, beginning to spread through the room. The young teacher was staring wildly about her, trying to decide where it came from – or which of them it came from. Eventually her nose led her to the culprit and, beneath Lucky's interested scrutiny, she underwent a severe test of her resolve.

To begin with the teacher was equal to the task. At this stage she was still thinking logically, with a degree of confidence, and thus it was not unnatural that she should consider the behaviour of the boy Seraphim to be somehow a challenge to her authority, an attempt to disrupt the class which she must resist for the sake of maintaining order in the future. So she opened several windows and continued to distribute blocks of writing paper, sharpened pencils and thick yellow rubbers. 'I must press on,' she told herself. Seraphim, however, was constituting his reply to this clear but superficial thinking which presumed African affairs to be susceptible to this sort of commonsense; or, put another way, Seraphim proceeded to expose the seemingly understandable European desire to move forward steadily in a proper fashion as being nothing more than the wish to compel and command. Very deliberately he reached into the back of his baggy khaki shorts and smeared a handful of excrement slowly into his hair. It looked, at least to Lucky, like a gesture both unanswerable and somehow magnificent.

This was only the first of a series of sharp lessons the German teacher learnt in the school-room at the back of the Lutheran Mission. She had, for a start, no option but to recall the black assistant whom she had rejected and this calm and pleasant lady led Seraphim away and cleaned him up. In the confusion the schizophrenic girl stabbed one of the boys with her sharpened pencil, puncturing a major vein in his thigh, and he had to be rushed to the huge black hospital on the edge of the township. Amid the howls and noisy convulsions the little girl China lay down on the floor, drew her knees up to her chin, screwed her eyes even more tightly shut and stuck her thumb in her mouth.

It was not unnatural, perhaps, that Ilse should mention to the doctor her fears about the aggressive behaviour of the schizophrenics. They were proving extremely disruptive in class. The doctor promised action. Within days she noticed a radical change in the behaviour of all three: the stabbed boy, his thigh swathed in a large white tubular bandage, his would-be assassin and the other lad changed from moody, violent children into dreamy creatures who sleepwalked through the day. If they were no longer a problem, they were also out of her reach. They attended her classes like ghosts and it was only when her alarm led her again to the doctor that she discovered the explanation. The doctor from Cologne had arranged a course of treatment for the children at the big hospital down the road, an experimental mixture of electrotherapy and drugs which had been shown to have very promising effects in a number of trial programmes in Europe. The doctor was enthusiastic about the programme and seemed so sure of its beneficial effects on the children that Ilse could hardly object when she suggested they might be happier if they were transferred to the hospital as full-time patients. The doctor took her there as part of her general introduction to the country. It was, she said, one of the wonders of the Southern Hemisphere. It was run according to the highest medical standards and was far advanced by comparison with anything available in the so-called independent black African states to the north. These states, said the doctor from Cologne with a mixture of exasperation and regret which Ilse was coming to recognise and to dislike, had destroyed the medical infrastructures bequeathed to them by their former colonial masters just as wantonly as they had destroyed sensible veterinary precautions against spreading foot and mouth disease among livestock, or measures to combat the tsetse-fly.

'It's all very well to talk of freedom. But should you allow a person the freedom to commit suicide? When you've been in the country as long as I have you'll find that these are difficult questions to answer.' The doctor made a point of showing her the paraplegic ward. It was remarkable for the numbers of young cripples it contained.

'Most of these young men are victims of gang feuding, or common assaults by thugs who are after their pay packets. In their cases the weapon used is peculiar to the township. It is very deadly and yet homely: a bicycle spoke, sharpened to a point. When inserted into the spinal column, the result is permanent paralysis of the lower half of the body.'

'Then is there nothing to be done for these poor people, ever?' The girl was appalled.

'Nothing. However, you'll see we keep them busy. A number of good ladies from one of the charitable organisations in the city come here once a week and teach them crafts. It's useful therapy.'

Many of the young cripples were knitting. The click of their needles was the only sound in the large sunny ward. It was a strange sight, these husky young men with their big muscles, their knife scars, their broken noses, sitting patiently knitting, frowning ferociously over a V-necked sweater or frantically searching for a dropped stitch in a baby's pink bootee.

'What you must understand is that crimes of the white man against the black don't compare with the violence of black against black,' said the doctor from Cologne. 'It's not simply a question of justice. Of course the racial phobias here are absurd. But, on the other hand, you can see their point. Why hand over yourself and all you have built here to be wrecked and ruined? Anyway the real problems, between you and me, have nothing to do with race. Skin colour is really a side issue in Africa. The real problems here are drought and soil erosion; locusts; too many babies. You will understand this when you have been here as long as me.'

Perhaps, thought Ilse, that kind of understanding should be guarded against. For if these were the conclusions you came to when you saw the solutions to local failings and foolishness more clearly than the natives themselves, and if all you could dream of was real coffee again and European shade and green trees, then maybe there was a case for not staying too long, possibly a case for not coming at all. But of course she said none of this.

Her classes continued to deteriorate. Seraphim had gone for good and could be seen walking in the Mission garden attended by the black assistant. He no longer wore trousers or shoes and moved across the grass slowly, like an elderly casualty of some forgotten war. The schizophrenic children were so heavily drugged that they slept most of the morning and were barely conscious when they awoke. Ilse abandoned formal teaching; there was no teaching to be done. The only progress that she had made was with little China, whom she had cuddled and mothered until the child consented to get to her feet and open her eyes. She trailed along by Ilse's side, clinging to her skirt, thumb in her mouth, breathing heavily and hissingly through her nose.

Lucky paged through the reading books, ignoring words but falling with delight on pictures of giants and dragons. He came to her one day with a new picture. She looked at it. A ballet dancer pirouetted.

'Does it hurt? Lucky demanded in his own voice.

She explained that the dancers trained for this and they wore special shoes.

'Can she fly?' Lucky asked.

Ilse said no, she could not fly.

'Yes she can, my dear madam,' Lucky contradicted her in his Doctor Paul voice.

Ilse shook her head. Dancers did not fly. They leapt.

'Leapt?' Lucky was mystified.

Gently disengaging China from her skirt, Ilse gathered herself on her toes and leaped for the astonished Lucky.

'Again!' commanded the boy. 'That sure looks good, honey child.' Lucky spoke in the foolish inept twang of the radio cowboy.

How she hated these cheap disguises. She looked long and hard at the boy. So piercing, cold and foreign was her look that he flushed darkly and rolled his eyes at the ceiling. 'Again!'

'Who is asking me?'

He jabbed his thumb into his chest. 'Me. Lucky.'

'Then let me hear Lucky speak in his own voice.'

The boy gave her a look in which truculence was mixed with fear. He did not like this cold distant tone, this harsh steely demeanour. 'Please,' he said in his own light, high voice. 'Again!'

She retreated into the corner of the room while China looked on nervously. Kicking off her shoes and holding her skirt above her knees, she ran forward and soared into the air, brushing the light with her outstretched hand.

Lucky gave a roar of delight in which there was to be heard joy mingled with relief. Here at last was a person who did things herself. How many had he known whom he had had to put through their paces? To lift them up? Make them fly? Turn them into goats, or snails or snakes? For most people, he knew, could do nothing for themselves and it was he who would have to make them disappear, or crawl on their bellies, or explode in a thousand pieces – anything that made them be something other than the hateful, familiar frowning creatures who shouted at him or threw stones. How many had he sent away? Killed would be the true word for it. But he did not like that word. Extinguished them with a glance, with a thought. Now here at last was someone with her own magic. A bird woman. He clapped his hands until they stung and tears ran down his face. He was joined by China, alarmed by the commotion, who ran to Ilse weeping and buried her face in her lap.

It was a few days after this that China fell ill. Ilse stayed with her throughout the night, but she did not improve. She had a high fever and diarrhoea. The doctor was called and diagnosed amoebic dysentery. In the morning she would be admitted to hospital. Ilse sitting by the child's bed with cool towels and cups of water, did what she could to lower the fever and waited for the morning.

In the morning China was dead.

Ilse came to the classroom where only Lucky faced her, brilliant with admiration for the displays of the day before. She hated his glowing anticipation.

'I cannot teach today. China died last night.'

Lucky thought for a time, his face showing no emotion.

'I am glad,' he said in his own voice after a long while.

29

The air turned solid and pressed on her and she heard a rubbery drumming in her ears. She moved towards him with difficulty; the air which had been solid suddenly receded before her and she was swimming in a hot black mist in which all she could see was her raised hand. She knew she was going to hit him. Again and again. She wanted to kill him.

Lucky knew it and he did not flinch. He waited, completely unmoved. It was his silent acceptance that stayed her hand. She knew, she saw, he did not care. Blows would not move Lucky. She felt bitterly ashamed.

'But why? Why glad?'

Again Lucky considered the question carefully. 'Because, honey child,' he drawled in his cowboy accent, 'she's gone somewhere.'

'She's dead, Lucky. That's not a trip. It's not a place you visit.'

Lucky shrugged. 'It's not here. It's somewhere else, isn't it?'

And that was how she came to teach Lucky. In part because he would not be moved. In part because he was all she had left. But also because she felt she had failed him. Lucky, she realised, took a view of things so bleak that she could not even begin to comprehend it. Then there was also the fact that, as she privately admitted to herself, she desired some kind of success. The thought of utter failure after so short a time, of the waste and wreck of her dreams, was too much to bear.

THREE

Hunch, weapon, inspiration, experiment, surprise – it was all of these as well as a demonstration of certain cultural and technical abilities. It was also, quite simply, a 16 mm film – shot in colour – of the ballet *Swan Lake*. She had ordered it from Germany. The projector she obtained from the German Club, loyal patron of the Lutheran Mission, where they regarded the new teacher as having admirable progressive ideas about the education of disadvantaged children.

'I will tell you the story as we go along.'

'Like the football,' said Lucky, 'on the radio.'

'This is not football. And it is nothing like the radio. Watch, listen and you will see.'

'It's a film,' Lucky declared with what he hoped was decent insolence. 'I have seen films before. We have them here, in the Social Centre. Many films.'

The fact was that he had watched her setting up the equipment with growing astonishment. Was there nothing this woman could not do? He was overwhelmed not only by the cool efficiency with which she threaded the spool of film into the machine, checked and adjusted the wheels, buttons and switches, but also by her transformation of the room into a cinema in five minutes. The door had been locked, the curtains drawn, the projector propped on a Phillips atlas and when that wasn't sufficient, on a Bible as well. He had never seen books better used. The Bible was so fat and packed with thousands of black bodies which swarmed like sugar ants and made his head swim. In the atlas he had been shown the map of South Africa but found it impossible to believe Ilse when she insisted that this flat brown stain, veined like an old leaf, was his homeland. It looked like nothing on earth. And then, yes, the screen which for the life of him he could not see, suddenly appeared! She produced it literally from nowhere. Ilse put her shoulder to the large stationery cupboard and it slid into the corner without protest, exposing the glorious white wall, the perfect screen on which she was now testing her focus. The power and perfection of the organisation she brought to bear on the room astounded him. To find it so easy to make things happen, to get things done, just like that!

'Whsshtwhsst . . .' Lucky blew through his lips and shook his head. He shivered. Though of course he would not show it. Ilse had a cold power that came from the outside and made things happen. Cut through difficulties. No one he knew had anything like it – not the cops, nor the sharp men who ran the township, nor the white men from the city who seemed to Lucky much more like bears than men. He watched them driving around, thick hair bunching on their chests and legs – untidy, sweaty, dusty, irritable creatures who yelled a lot and barged into things. These people were heavy and ugly and stupid. The girl was not like that. She was like a knife.

'I have been to movies. Oh yes, often.'

It was a lie. The closest he had been to a cinema screen was twenty metres away, crouching in the darkness outside the Bantu Men's Social Centre after the doors were closed, the tough men and their dolls were safely inside and you could watch a reflection of the film in the dirty window of Peejay Stores. From the dim verandah of the Stores you watched the distorted reflection of a thin section of the screen, slices of light in which there appeared hats, noses, guns, lips, teeth. All quite silent, of course.

'What film is this? Cowboys? Gangsters?'

Her answer was to flick the light switch and plunge him into the brown and yellow darkness of an African afternoon with the sun beating on the curtains. Upon the wall of the classroom where the stationery cupboard had stood there appeared now a magnificent red velvet curtain as high, surely, as the green neon cross on the roof of the Adventist Church? Slowly the curtain parted, lifted and disappeared up into the roof, and there in front of him was a deep dark green forest. Standing in a clearing were frozen figures – girls in pretty skirts and the men wearing the most wonderful high boots Lucky had ever seen. And there in the far corner was a castle. It had towers, battlements and little hats for roofs, and a light, yes!, a light in an upper window where doubtless a Princess waited for someone, perhaps for Lucky, to save her from the giant downstairs. Frantically, like a fat boy in a sweetshop, Lucky crammed the pictures into his mind lest the show stop. Now there was music. The figures sprang to life and they were dancing. Like she had danced. Oh, it was a dream!

'Lucky!' Her outraged voice burnt in his ears.

'Yes, miss.'

'You mustn't scream. People will wonder what is going on here.'

'Miss?'

'Look, here is the Prince now.'

'What is his name?'

'His name is Siegfried.'

'Zeegfreed.' He pronounced it carefully, buzzingly. 'Thank you, miss.'

Shamefaced, he covered his lips with his hands. He had not been aware of his scream. Through his fingers now he observed the Prince with keen interest. Tall and supple like bamboo, he wore on his head a thin gold coronet.

'Why does he walk on his toes?'

'They all walk that way, the women especially. High on their toes. They're not really walking, they're dancing. Everything moves all the time in the dance. Like a river. Or the wind.'

'They are very happy,' Lucky said.

'It is the Prince's birthday and they're having a big party.'

'Who is the old man in the skins?'

'The Prince's teacher. He is a learned man and those are his professor clothes. He doesn't want the Prince to waste time; he wants him to work hard and be serious.'

'I don't like him. The old teacher does not walk on his toes. He sways.' Lucky gave a great shout of laughter and immediately again clasped his hands to his lips. 'Sorry, sorry! But I think the teacher is drunk, drunk . . . he's been too long at the beer hall.'

Lucky grew very agitated when the drunken teacher attempted a few steps with one of the village girls. 'Leave her alone, old fool!' And then fell utterly silent as he witnessed the presentation of a crossbow to the Prince.

'Prince Siegfried likes the bow. He likes the bow better than the girls,'   *33*

Ilse explained. 'But his mother, the Queen, is very strict. She says to him that tomorrow there will be a big dance and there he must choose a wife from among the princesses . . .'

'I think he must go hunting if that is what pleases him,' Lucky insisted.

If the first act excited Lucky, the second shocked and exhilarated him so profoundly that she thought she might have to stop the film. At his first glimpse of the party of huntsmen who came to carry off the Prince into the forest, Lucky clapped loudly. When the swans appeared, Ilse could hear him panting hugely. He half rose from his seat and mimicked the movement of their arms. Behind him, she kept up a gentle, calm commentary on the action. She told him of the magic lake, made of the tears wept by the mother of the Swan Girl, Odette. Swan by day, woman only at night, trapped for ever in the spell of an evil magician. A spell which could be broken only by someone who had never loved before. Then Odette arrived on stage, a feathered dream. Prince Siegfried lifted the crossbow.

'No, no,' Lucky shouted. 'Don't shoot!'

When Swan Girl and Prince started dancing together and the harp accompanied them, Lucky joined in. 'Plink, plonk, plink' he sang, completely out of tune. And when the solitary violin began, he rose from his chair and mimicked the action of the fiddler. When the evil Owl Magician, Rothbart, appeared suddenly in a swirling fluttering cloak of feathers upon his dark perch and menaced the swans, Lucky fell back into his chair, his hands raised, fingers crooked like the claws of some hunting cat.

'But why does the Prince not kill the wizard?' Lucky demanded in the deepest anguish. 'Shoot, shoot the owl!' he instructed the Prince through cupped hands.

'He cannot,' Ilse explained. 'Odette tells him that if the magician dies then the spell can never be broken and she will stay a swan for ever.'

Lucky ground his teeth in exasperation. 'Stupid!' he muttered.

So it went. The second appearance of the Queen caused another flurry of excitement in the boy, who insisted on rising to his feet, whether because he thought it proper in the presence of royalty or simply for a better view, Ilse did not know. She explained that the Queen was accompanied by six princesses. The number seemed impossibly rich to Lucky, who hugged himself in the darkness and muttered, 'Six, six, six' in a mixture of anguish and delight. He was aghast to hear that the Prince was permitted to choose one only and shouted at the screen, 'Take that one, with the yellow hair, or the little one with the flowers!' as the Prince dallied and fiddled in a disinterested way with his prospective fiancées. When the daughter of Rothbart, disguised as the true Swan Girl, dances for the Prince who falls in love with this false black swan, Lucky called loudly to the Prince warning him that the real swan stood grieving at the window, and again Ilse had to quieten him.

Finally, at the end when the lovers are joined together in death and sail across the stage escorted by a lamenting flotilla of swans, Lucky wept harsh noisy tears which he made no attempt to hide or staunch.

She turned on the lights. He was slumped in his chair with his eyes closed and for a moment she thought that he had fainted. When at last he spoke, he said only one word. 'Again.'

'All of it?' Ilse asked, half amused but with a faint tremor of doubt at the overwhelming success of her experiment.

'All,' Lucky replied, still without opening his eyes. It was as if he did not wish to lose the images dancing behind his eyelids.

They saw the film again and then every day that week. Control was what she desired; she recognised that later. The story, the film, the ballet were her way into the fantastical recesses of Lucky's mind. For if the boy was enthralled by his dreams, then perhaps the way to exert influence was to attempt to control those dreams. Let him see it as many times as he liked. Afterwards they would build on the story. She would help him to draw the Prince, the wicked Owl Sorcerer and the Lake and the Swans. She would teach him to write the names of the Prince and of the Swan Girl. Maybe they would count the Swans . . . slowly she would build up in Lucky a body of knowledge. In short, she would do what she had set out to do when she had landed in Africa. She would teach, she would do some good. She might have lost her pupils one by one, she realised that. But Lucky remained, and him she would not fail.

So she taught him. She stood on one leg, bent forward from the hips and extended her arms.

'Arabesque.'

35

'Ah!' The information clearly delighted him and he followed suit. She showed him how to turn; she demonstrated the pirouette and Lucky applauded so loudly her ears stung.

'Where do these people live?'

'The story is set in the south of Germany.'

'Where you come from.'

'Yes. But it all takes place long, long ago.'

'And the people who dance – are they film stars?'

'No. They are ballet dancers.'

'Yes. But what else do they do?'

'Nothing else.'

'Paid to dance?' Lucky gave way to hysterical laughter. 'No, no, miss, you mustn't tell lies to Lucky.'

She did her best to convince him, but he laughed again and changed the subject. He began singing snatches of the overture. He had the most extraordinary memory for reproducing things recently heard. After successive showings of the film he sang tunefully as well. He was particularly good at mimicking the individual instruments and he enjoyed the sound of the harp. However, it was the violin that he particularly liked to recall, not only reproducing its sound but swaying from the waist with a dreamy expression on his face as he stroked his imaginary fiddle, turning and bowing and interspersing his performance with clumsy little ballet steps. It was this that gave Ilse her second idea. Once again she approached her sponsors, the German Club, with an unusual request. To Lucky she said nothing yet. In any event, he could talk about nothing but the story of the ballet.

'How many years that mother must have cried, *cried* for her daughter. To fill a whole lake! Is that lake as big as ours?' He was referring to the dusty strip of water in the dip, covered with a film of dust where the milk bottles floated.

'Bigger.'

He shook his head in amazement. 'We have no swans on our lake. Not even ducks. But this is good. Yes. People would kill them.'

Ilse said she was sure no one would kill a swan.

Lucky stared at her as if she were mad. A little later he asked rather diffidently about the role of the Black Swan, the imposter Odile.

'She is the daughter of the wizard. She tricks the Prince, who is bewitched by Rothbart. The Prince thinks the Black Swan is really the White Swan, Odette.'

He smiled grimly. 'Black swans can be clever. Full of magic.'

He was now much more relaxed in her company. They began to take long walks through the township in the afternoons. It was on one of these walks that he returned, as he so often did, to the subject of the film. 'Can even black people dance in these ballets?'

'Of course.'

He stopped walking and seized her hand in his excitement. 'Then I will go there. Overseas. Where anyone can dance. What must I do, to tell them?'

'You will say to the people there: "My name is Lucky. I wish to learn to dance."'

The terrible simplicity of this seemed to strike him in the heart. 'Maybe, maybe. Perhaps one day.'

'I'm sure you will, Lucky, one day.'

Suddenly he seemed to resent her tone, as if he suspected she was patronizing him. 'No, I will go soon.' He lowered his voice. 'Did you know that I can fly? Like a bird? Like . . .' he paused for emphasis, '. . . like a swan.'

'Oh Lucky, Lucky!' was all she could say in her pain and frustration and near despair. For increasingly she was aware of the gap opening between what she could give him there and then, and Lucky's implacable desire to be off, somewhere, anywhere, elsewhere.

Yet her plan seemed to be working, for in the classroom they drew swans and owls and crossbows; they lettered the names of each of these and learnt them by heart. He managed to count up to six swans. She was distressed that a boy well into his teens could neither read nor count and she was determined as a teacher to provide remedies. She had already achieved some small successes. He no longer used his variety of radio voices and spoke now only in his own dry, piping tones. Yet she sensed something of a lack of interest in the purely educational side of her project. He did not really care for the pictures unless they moved and were accompanied by music. He sang as he drew but the drawings were bad, he chanted as he counted but the numbers were not consecutive, and when he did neither of these things she found him hopping across the classroom on his toes. Where he seemed happiest

37

was in their walks around the township and she began to wonder whether he had not perhaps decided that it was time to teach her something, for certainly he increasingly took the lead, seemingly oblivious to the stir they caused.

They would have been noticed, a white woman and a black boy walking through the township, even if it had not been that Lucky seemed to set out to attract attention.For example, there was his new costume. He had found for himself, heaven alone knew where, a pair of leggings which probably had once been baseball trousers, or perhaps they were jodphurs; at any rate they reminded Ilse of the short trousers which clamped below the knee and were favoured by walkers in her native Germany. He wore as well a pair of old sandshoes, rather too large, to which many coats of whitener carefully applied had given an appearance of chalky, pristine splendour. Until, that is, he set off upon his walk, when the thick crust split to reveal old grey canvas beneath. He wore also his yo-yo tee-shirt from which the Coca-Cola logo had been obliterated beneath a layer of the same white shoe cream. His outfit declared to all that here was Lucky the ballet dancer – Lucky as Prince Siegfried. And if anyone failed to realise this, then he made it very plain by pausing whenever the mood took him and performing arabesques in the dusty street while mimicking Tchaikovsky's music.

If Lucky was oblivious to the amusement he caused in passers-by, then Ilse was not. She heard and felt their consternation, though it caused her no more than a faint pang of embarrassment on Lucky's behalf. She had no idea what lay behind their wonderment. One day they had walked for about a mile and interest had been particularly intense. They had gone uphill to the railway line, turned left at the Af-mark dealer, passed Barclays Bank, where several customers actually came out to gawp at the thin prancing boy in his white clothes and his very black arms and legs. They went on past Uncle Tom's Hall, turned right at the power station where Lucky changed his mind and turned left to pass the beer hall with its sour, yeasty smell and its dazed old men sitting outside in the winter sunshine. Admiring the witch-doctor's modern house, they turned left again to go under the railway line and came to a stretch of dark water filmed with dust. At one end stood a group of very old weeping willows trailing their branches in the water, looking to her like women turning their heads away. At the other side

was a small crop of green reeds. The banks of the little lake were muddy and dirty with rubbish: a pink nightdress, a boot without a sole, a sodden comic book of Superman which she had trouble persuading Lucky to leave where it was. An old oil-drum, almost submerged, bobbed in the water.

'You see, there are no ducks,' Lucky said. 'They would eat them,' he jerked a thumb over his shoulder.

'Surely not!'

'Of course. People are hungry. They would eat anything. Even swans.'

'Then it is good there are none here.'

But Lucky was not to be put off. 'They would come here at night and catch the swan. They would put it in the pot and cook it. They would eat it all up!' Lucky demonstrated how the bird's neck would be wrung and then he chewed noisily and smacked his lips.

She could not get over the lake. Why put it here? She asked him what the lake was for. Lucky looked decidedly shifty and glared at the bobbing oil-drum, a curved gleam on the water, like a hippo's back.

'People even eat cats.'

'Lucky, stop! Do not say any more. Let's go on with our walk.'

'They use their skins for hats,' said Lucky.

Now they arrived at the tarred road which formed the eastern boundary of the township and led to the white city somewhere in the blue distance. Beside the road was an enormous hoarding on steel supports and in its shade they rested.

She knew of Lucky's admiration for huge pictures of smiling men. Early in their friendship he had pointed out the advertising poster for *Lucky Strike* cigarettes, with its picture of his secret father. He had confessed to her his theory that he and the strong, smiling man were related. She had no doubt, looking at his tense beatific expression, that he believed this to be so and she readily agreed not to reveal his secret. Then also there had been his walking, talking transmission of favourite radio programmes, any and all of them, – something which it seemed he had at last outgrown – as well as the way in which he had blossomed so extraordinarily when shown the film of *Swan Lake*. He was, she supposed, a child of his time, enormously and naturally influenced by the public media. She would not have been surprised if, in another country, he might have displayed a natural talent for radio or film; he was so clearly born to it. Except of course that this was out of the question. There *was* no other time and place for Lucky. Even so, it amused her to speculate on what he would have done in the outside world. The fact that he was illiterate would not have harmed his chances. In Europe, she reflected, he would probably have become a television producer.

Ilse was surprised, therefore, to see him jump on the metal upright at the base of the huge hoarding and begin to pull at the paper. The hoarding seemed to her to advertise some political campaign. It carried the large letters NP in blue and orange and was dominated by the fleshy, neatly groomed grey head of a middle-aged man who looked faintly familiar.

She was unhappy to see Lucky tearing at the poster; she recoiled from such vandalism.

'Please, don't do that.'

'When my Granny Muriel comes here, when she goes past this picture she spits. Everyone spits. Do you know this man? He is called the Doctor.'

Ilse examined the Doctor. She wished she knew more about the country. But in Germany they took no interest in the place. Many people thought she must be going to one of the old German colonies when she said she was going to South Africa. The Doctor's face was solid and rectangular, with plump high cheeks and wavy grey hair cut short at the sides. He was smiling faintly and this gave him an air of benignity that persisted until she looked into the light blue eyes which were small and rather narrow. The kindly air faded as she studied the eyes staring out above her head towards the dusty darkness of the dirty slick of water called the township lake. It was a curious face in which the dreamy quality of the equable visionary combined with the rock-like determination of the fanatic.

'My Granny says the Doctor wants to eat us.'

'Why should a doctor want to eat people, Lucky?'

Lucky cocked an imaginary crossbow and aimed at the man's right eye. 'Pow! Pow!' The look he gave her was full of hot, angry desperation.

'Please, no talk of eating. Come down.'

41

Lucky shrugged and stripped off a piece of the man's jaw, coming close to cutting through his peach-pink and dimpled cheek. It was only when she promised him a special surprise if he came back to the school with her that he could be persuaded to jump down from the railing. She felt very relieved he was down when she saw the grey police van come cruising down the road. She took his hand and led him away. Just in time, she thought.

But the sight of the boy and girl walking hand in hand was in itself startling enough to send the police van dangerously close to skidding into a ditch. It was, to say the least, unusual. And what was unusual in the township was almost always illegal. It is certain that the German teacher had no idea of the effect she created, though she was aware that the people in the township laughed at Lucky and if it had been at all possible, she would have liked to spare him ridicule. Of other inferences about her behaviour she knew nothing. After all, she was from Germany and her German innocence kept her from knowing what was going on. As for Lucky, had he thought about it at all, he would not have cared less.

A few days later she gave him a violin, a gift based upon a wide variety of impulses. Above all it had seemed to her a sensible thing to do, an effective way of showing some recognition of his evident desires and talents. Since it was quite clear to her that his love of radio and film would not, *could* not lead him anywhere and since the idea of becoming a dancer, though it might have seemed a pretty and beguiling notion was, when she thought about it, absolutely, even grotesquely impossible in his present circumstances, so the fiddle seemed perhaps the way to proceed. She had seen how deeply he responded to the music of *Swan Lake* and it occurred to her how wonderful it would be if she had, by the happiest of chances, stumbled across someone with a natural bent for music-making. She had noted how uncannily he could recall and reproduce the sound of the harp, flute and violin, to which the Swan Girl and the Prince danced together. The violin was another donation from her friends in the German Club. They had been amazed by her assertion that she might have found in the township a pupil who could study the violin with profit. Such a thing had never happened there before. Certainly children in the township had been given music lessons, but on instruments for which there was a demand and also a certain logic, like the saxophone, the drums and even the piano. But that was jazz, of course. Nonetheless they were impressed and excited and an inexpensive violin was duly obtained in a green case with a block of pink resin and a bow strung with a shank of the whitest horsehair.

Lucky was entranced and fell upon the instrument with whoops of joy. He tucked it beneath his chin. He plucked a high note on the E-string, played a long dark note on the G-string and then mimicked his favourite section of the ballet where the Prince seeks the girl amongst the Swans, cannot find her for a few panic-stricken moments while the harp becomes agitated, and then suddenly the Swans disclose the girl, the violin begins and Prince and Swan Maiden melt together in the dance.

'Yes, yes,' she encouraged him. 'Maybe one day, if you learn, you can play this. Really. Like the orchestra.'

Lucky, emboldened, drew the bow across all four strings and stopped dead, appalled by the discordancy. 'Go on. You can learn,' Ilse urged.

Learn was the word, of course – the one she did not mention even to herself. Yet she knew that the idea behind the fiddle was, like all her ideas, educational. It was part of her determination as a teacher that her last remaining pupil should be taught something. Determination was closely linked with duty – so closely that they were really indistinguishable. She could see him already, taking his first lesson from some old violinist who played Austrian Ländler at the German Club. Simple little tunes to start with. But then, later, Mozart perhaps – who could say?

Again he drew the bow across the strings. The sound was very ugly. He lowered the fiddle; it seemed to him that the instrument was wicked. He heard the music in his head, but all the violin said was, 'Fool!' It mocked him. It screamed and howled. It blocked out the real music. It perched on his shoulder and laughed at him. Perhaps for the very first time in his life he felt weak, contemptible, despised. He held the fiddle by its pegs, swinging it against his thigh. Where it touched his skin he felt its evil charm, heard the hollow boom of its wooden laughter.

Ilse grieved. She moved towards him with her arms open.

But she was too late. Swiftly he lifted the fiddle and brought it down across the edge of the desk. It broke at the neck and swung by its strings,

43

giving a deep strangled cough when it bumped against the leg of the desk. It looked quite horribly like a dead bird . . . a chicken with its neck wrung.

'I have killed the Wizard! Rothbart is dead!'

She knew then that she had failed. There was nothing left to teach Lucky. So she spoke to him in the only language he appeared to understand.

'You shouldn't have done that. Don't you remember what I told you? If the Prince kills the owl, then the spell can never be broken and the girl must stay a swan always. And that violin was a gift of good, kind people. What must I tell them?'

In reply Lucky threw the broken fiddle into the corner and tossed the bow after it. 'Dead,' he repeated defiantly.

It seemed to her then that she had reached the bottom of the pit. However, as the events of the next few hours were to show dramatically, she had still a long way to descend. For it was only then that she had truly arrived in Africa. And in those few moments she grew, she aged. She felt it happening to her. Certainly, it was an older and tougher Ilse who turned on her heel and left the classroom, slamming the door behind her without a backward glance at the boy who sat in the rear desk with his head buried in his arms. There burned in her a feeling of anger and defiance which she felt would carry her through anything.

The next morning a letter arrived in a heavy brown envelope bearing a government crest. It was simply phrased and to the point.

> *The Minister has decided that it is not in the public interest*
> *to renew your visa permitting you to take employment in*
> *the Republic. You are hereby instructed to make arrange-*
> *ments to leave the country within seventy-two hours.*

She sent the letter to the doctor from Cologne, who summoned her to an urgent meeting. Waiting in the doctor's outer office, Ilse sat opposite a small, frail but fierce little woman in a most agitated state. She hissed to herself like a heating pot and muttered and frowned. Every now and then she smashed a fist into her palm. The glance she gave Ilse was full of loathing; she almost spat. But the girl barely noticed her emotion and did not recognise Lucky's Granny, Muriel. The doctor called Ilse into her office and although the little black woman protested that she had been there first, the doctor was adamant.

Once seated at her desk, the doctor lost no time. 'This is a disaster. I must telephone friends.'

Ilse must have shown her surprise because the doctor added, 'My friends have friends in the government.'

First she spoke to someone whom she approached in the most casual terms asking about family and friends. She next spoke to someone else about rugby, the weather and the shooting season. Eventually she mentioned in the same cheerful tones the deportation order. Her friend spoke for some time while the doctor listened, still with the smile of artificial breeziness. Even after she had replaced the receiver, the smile died slowly.

'It seems that there have been reports. The order was issued as a result. Never before in the Mission have we had such a report.'

The notion of the 'reports' appeared to give her peculiar joy because she dwelt heavily on the two syllables of the word, nodding significantly as she did so.

'My friends say nothing can be done. This will damage us. And our work here. Damage the children.'

Ilse was puzzled. 'But I want you to help me. You will support me? How can they just tell me to leave?'

'This,' said the doctor wearily, waving a hand at the township beyond the window, 'is South Africa.'

'What are these reports?' Ilse demanded.

'And in South Africa there are very serious rules. People can be jailed who do not obey.'

'I do not know what you mean.'

'I presume even you know that it is against the law for a white person to have relationships with a black?'

'Yes, I know that.'

'You may not agree with it. But when in Rome we do as the Romans do. Not so? Personally I do not agree with this mystification of the blood which these people go in for. But we are guests here. Well now, what do you say?'

'To what?'

45

'To the reports that you have a more than professional relationship with one of your pupils.'

Ilse stared. 'Who makes these reports?'

'The police.'

'Are you saying that I've . . .' But she could not say the word. 'With Lucky!' And she began to laugh. It was the first time in many months, perhaps in years that she had laughed so freely.

'Are you mad?' The doctor leaped from her desk, seized Ilse's shoulders and shook them hard. 'Why do you laugh? Stupid girl? What have you done?'

Ilse struggled free of her grasp. 'Because it's not true!'

The doctor let her head sink closer and closer to Ilse's. Her neck was brown and wrinkled, with a ridge of down running along the faintly freckled nape. Her hair was sparse and deep lines bracketed her pinched lips. Now she laughed a dry, bitter, rusty little chuckle.

'You understand nothing about this place. You have been here five minutes; you have lost all your pupils except one, and him you have ruined by your behaviour. In a day or two you will be back in Germany. Home! And still you will have understood nothing. What does it matter if it is true or not? It is in the police reports. They say you slept with the boy. That is all that matters. The boy's grandmother is here. She gave him to us so that we could help him. What am I going to say to her?'

Before Ilse could think of a reply the door opened and Lucky's Granny, Muriel, entered at a run. She danced from one foot to the other while sizing up the two women and then flew at the doctor.

'You took my Lucky to this place. My boy who is mad, with his head full of rubbish. You said it would be okay. Muriel gave him to you so you can make him better. But he is not better. Lucky is mad. More mad than ever he was before. He runs around like a bird. He says he can fly! He dances in the street where people see him. They see him and they laugh. He tells them he is going soon. Overseas! He is going far, far away. He is going overseas because overseas everyone is free and can dance and do what they like. Even black people. This, the teacher tells him. She!' Muriel wheeled and pointed an accusing finger at Ilse.

'Please . . .' She wanted to explain.

'Go!' instructed the doctor. 'Say nothing. It is too late. The best of our dreams are broken.' Her look softened fractionally. 'It happens here.

How could you know? It's this place; it's in a different category. You have been too innocent.'

Ilse wandered back to the classroom. She felt hot and cold; her temples were icy, her palms burnt. That both women should consider her an ignorant foreigner out of her depth – foolish, childish, rash and thoughtless – made her giddy with shame and horror. They were right, of course, up to a point. They knew how things worked here. But it was a knowledge she despised. She remembered the police van following them on the day Lucky had attacked the poster. Yes, she had been too innocent. She had not thought; she was guilty of the thought that had not occurred to her.

Lucky sat where she had left him, slumped on a desk with his head in his arms. She closed the door and locked it, drew the curtains just as she had done when they had watched the film together. Then she switched off the lights. In the brown and yellow darkness she saw Lucky sit up and take notice. Her head felt light and she could not control her legs which shook and trembled. She began pushing the desks out of the way and they banged together in the darkness. Lucky watched silently. When she had cleared a space she began, very deliberately, to remove her dress. Beneath it she wore a white brassiere and pants. She kicked off her shoes and then, raising herself on her toes, she began to dance. She knew he understood because from the dark corner where he sat, the harp began its melody, announcing that the Prince was searching for his love. Then the violin climbed dreamily from the darkness, moved towards her and they were dancing together. To Lucky it was magic. The dream had happened. He lifted her and she did not object. Her skin was cool and fresh. He carried her as he had seen the Prince carrying the Swan Girl. He was strong enough to do it. And proud to do it. He lifted her above his head and she flowed, like milk pouring from a bottle, her waist bending like the wind's.

It was she who first felt the tension between them. Perhaps only because she was older. Certainly not because she was more experienced. Her experiences with Boris had been rather like immersing herself in a calm, rather tepid sea. But she recognised what was happening. Lucky's knowledge of these things would have been slight and his experiences were so entwined with his dreams and imaginings, with radio programmes and pictures, that he could hardly be described

47

as well-versed. So it was she who felt the tension . . . felt him stiffen as he clung to her. For her part she flowed with him, rode along, made no objection when she felt his hands on her breasts, when he found the clip to her brassiere and when he pressed his head against her breasts as if he were listening to her heart. It was she who helped him out of his ridiculously tight-fitting jodphurs, who drew him down beside her, who slipped her pants below her knees and drew him on to her while the boy's breath beat wildly in her ear. She cried hard, once, when he entered. Then they were sailing, and this time she carried him. Lucky, to his immense surprise at being carried so easily, so flowingly partnered, tried desperately to imagine in colours, since he could find no pictures, what he was feeling as he rose and fell above the girl who beat her arms in the darkness, white and glimmering. She was glad. All through it she wanted to shout with gladness. It had come too late, but it had come: a small thing saved against the wreck of her short career in the township. One thing learnt, about rules in particular. There were some which you did not study, or obey, or did not believe people when they said about them that they were no joke. What you did with rules like that was straightforward: you made every effort, as soon as possible, to break them.

FOUR

She had given him the film. Three heavy reels packed into tin boxes and lashed together with a red leather belt, from which the colour was flaking in the same way as the red paint puckered and peeled on the roof of the Bantu Men's Social Centre, into which Lucky would un-expectedly step at a slow march some days later, lifting his feet in the goose-step. The march had been demonstrated to him by Ilse in an effort to explain to him the nature of the war in Germany and her father's role in it. But he had not understood her explanation. To her amazement he did not know of the war she talked about so angrily. He had never heard of Hitler. However, he did a fine impersonation of Nazi soldiers on parade. Lucky's talent for mimicry and impersonation filled her with despair; he flowed into whatever frame or situation he was offered. She had taken his thin face and pressed it between her hands, making him look her in the eyes.

'When will you stop being other things? Other people? Who will look after you when I am gone?'

There, it was out.

Lucky eyed her as if she were making a joke. 'Let us see the film again.'

'I must go back to Germany.'

Lucky smiled brilliantly. 'I know Germany.'

He gently stroked the flesh of her upper arm above the elbow. She watched his fingers brushing her flesh, as if he were smoothing feathers. She could tell from his grimaces, the rolling eyes, the incessant pulling at his lip, that his thoughts must have been frightened and agitated, but at last the long interior search of his mind provided him with the answer he wanted. He tapped his head.

'I come too.'

'No, Lucky. I must go alone. In the big aeroplane. Flying.'

His smile grew happier, broader, He spread his arms. 'Flying! I can do it!'

She tried not to cry. She was determined not to weep. 'I've got a present for you.' She gave him the heavy cans of film in their red leather strap that still smelt of the cowhide from which it had been cut. 'You must keep this for me. It's the film of the Swan. For you, for ever.'

Lucky received the gift calmly and studied his toes for some time. When he lifted his head the look he gave her was surprisingly cunning.

'When are you going to Germany?'

She fell into the trap. 'Today. Now.'

His relief was palpable. 'Then we will watch the film tomorrow, when you come back. I keep this until tomorrow.' He hugged the cans to his chest.

She kissed his forehead. 'Goodbye.'

'Tomorrow,' he said.

When Lucky presented himself at the Lutheran Mission on the following day, the doctor from Cologne threw him out. She was not naturally unkind, but amid the wreckage of her dreams of a haven for the mentally troubled there had emerged another grave problem. Earlier that morning she had endured an unpleasant encounter with the police, who had hinted at the most grotesque liaison between the former teacher and her pupil. Worse still, it seemed the teacher had not shown up for her flight. She had disappeared. Brutality seemed the only honest way of acting.

'The school is closed. Go home.'

Lucky rattled the film in the cans. 'I come to see the Swan. Where is the teacher?'

'Gone.'

'To Germany?'

'Gone, I say. Where are your shoes?'

Lucky contemplated his bare feet. It was a question he chose not to answer. The truth was that his Granny Muriel had taken his shoes, seized and burnt them in the black iron stove on which she cooked their meals. Into the flames went the sandshoes on which so many layers of whitener had been lavished that it crumbled from the old canvas in chalky fragments when he danced. Indeed, it had been in the belief, in the desperate hope that by destroying the shoes that Lucky would stop dancing, would cease to prance about the township, that Muriel had taken this drastic action.

Muriel feared terribly for Lucky.

She had good reason to be worried. People said things when they saw the boy – dark, hurtful things. They said things even when they did not see him, for his wild nimble progress about the township could be traced now by the streaks of chalk on the red ground. People would pause to examine these as if they were the baffling, arcane, magical spoor left by some fantastical animal.

People like Moses Nhlunga, the owner of the funeral parlour, spoke for many when in his slow cumbersome way he declared that Lucky's 'jumping foolishness', as he called it, was fit only for women and fools. It was not wise to ignore an undertaker's warning.

More dangerously, a number of local thugs took exception, and Two-Can Mafeti was their spokesman. He offered, in his silky and ominous way, to ease Muriel's suffering and pain by slicing off Lucky's toes, if that would help. A boy who declared his flagrant disregard for the facts of life by pussyfooting about the place like a bloody ballerina was not merely mad but 'a blot on the sweet face of his family and nation'. Two-Can told Muriel this while he stroked the bluish-purple weals of the old knife scars on his cheek, and his eyes misted over when he reflected on the old lady's suffering and her ungrateful grandson.

'That's not a boy, that's a Mexican jumping bean you've got there, Muriel. Say the word and I'll stand on him.'

But what disturbed Muriel most of all was the interest taken in Lucky by a man known only as the General. As it happened, the General had intervened when a crowd of boys had attacked Lucky with sticks for saying that one day everyone in the township would dance, because everyone would be free. When asked for substantiation of this foolish remark, Lucky replied that in the outside world everyone who wished to do so danced as much as they chose. Black people and white people danced together and everyone loved one another. The township boys laughed and asked if this meant that people who danced with one

51

another also screwed one another. And Lucky replied that of course it did. This was said with such quiet conviction that the boys laid into him with considerable violence and might very well have killed him for the crass, blinding, cheek of his reply – the huge, utterly sincere, horribly convincing lie – had the General not intervened.

Despite his name nothing about him suggested a military man. He was a little, balding and honey-coloured man who wore a pale grey fedora and had a way of bringing his hands together, first palm to palm, then finger to finger, and turning them over as if together they represented the sections of some beautiful and original puzzle which he had the supreme pleasure of owning and, alone, solving. He smiled as he did this, showing strong white teeth, yet there was an abstracted air about him, a carefully vague look in the eyes that suggested someone who spent most of the time laying his plans in his head and the rest of his time ensuring that he seemed as far away as he could possibly get from the dangerous martial character summed up in his nickname. Such was the General's reputation that when the boys beating Lucky saw him, they faltered and stopped. And when he picked Lucky up from the ground and dusted him off, the boys fled.

'Would you like to visit the outside world?' the General asked gently.

Lucky rubbed his knees to dislodge the sharp bits of flint which had stuck into the skin when the boys knocked him down. The blood ran down into his toes.

'I'm already going,' he announced proudly.

The General smiled. 'Where are you going?'

Lucky leaned down and rubbed his knees. The blood smeared his thin legs.

'To Germany. I will dance there.'

'And what would happen if someone tried to stop you? Would you fight them, Lucky?'

The boy considered this carefully. It had all the makings of a remarkable suggestion, one he had never thought of before. Why had he never thought of it before? He now fell to considering the question with such concentration that he quite forgot that an answer was expected.

When eventually he looked up again, the General was gone.

It was when she heard about the General's intervention that Muriel burnt the sandshoes. The incident terrified her. The man, she knew, had connections with mysterious people not only in the township, but much further away. People in the bush, across the border. His connections were so dangerous that no one spoke of them. They concerned movements by night, buried guns, blood. They ended in explosions, jail cells, scaffolds. Young men who fell in with the General disappeared from one night to the next. No letters arrived for their troubled parents. No reports of their whereabouts were ever received again. And when the police arrived asking questions, no one knew anything.

When the German doctor threw him out, Lucky turned on his bare heel and left the Lutheran Mission. He walked to the Bantu Men's Social Centre with his cans of film slung over his shoulder and there he put a proposition to the projectionist, Sam Mafekong – the fat, bitter Methodist.

Methodism was the projectionist's hope and dream, his cherished faith and lifelong consolation. Methodism taught Mafekong that a Christian must, as he follows Our Lord, take up his cross. He could not expect an easy ride. However, it was an inexplicable calamity in Sam's case that Christianity proved itself to be that cross. The conflict lay between his job and his faith. As a non-smoking, sweetly spoken teetotaller, he was obliged for his living to show movies of an unrelieved brutality and vulgarity to a collection of thugs, jailbirds and wideboys with knives in their pockets and blind worship in their hearts for the worst sort of Hollywood hoodlums. Saturday night was Mafekong's devil duty; he was the projectionist in Hell. While it was quite true that on Sundays he reaped his reward, not only in the morning when he preached in his church but in the evenings when he screened for a far smaller, older audience films of spiritual uplift, the clash between these two activities was greater than his faith could reconcile. Nonetheless he continued to show to ever dwindling audiences on Sunday nights short black and white films of English preachers with uncertain dentures who spoke of the heroism of John Wesley, preached from little chapels set among the valleys across which the rain drifted like grey smoke. Or he screened culturally valuable documentaries of the construction of hydro-electric schemes in Ontario. But he grew bitter. His dream was to show his Sunday films on Saturday nights. His dream was to do some

53

good. For he was an ambitious man. But he was also sensible and knew that pure religion would never sell. It was this which led him to the decision that perhaps culture might provide the link between the Saturday night devils and the good people of Sunday. Culture might provide the link – if only he could lay his hands on something which combined excitement and action with moral uplift. It had seemed to him at one time that the answer lay in Shakespeare. Specifically, in a film of *Macbeth* lent to him by a white charitable association in the city known as the Sons of the British Empire. Admittedly, he had been obliged to advertise the movie as being a story of the life and death struggle of a Scottish gang leader who rises to head his country's government – but this had been necessary to persuade people like Mr Ice and Two-Can Mafeti that, in their words, 'the celluloid was worth a run'. To convince them that it deserved a Saturday screening was no small achievement. But he also needed their reassurance that they would see to the behaviour of their friends. He got their reassurance; the audience would give the film a decent hearing, as Mafeti told him, or 'they get their lips sliced off'.

And indeed *Macbeth* was a great success; it caused a storm of approval. The audience were with the hero from the start. The murder of Duncan drew appreciative whistles and shouts of 'smart move, Mac!' Lady Macbeth's attempts to rally her husband after the assassination received equally warm support. 'You tell him, doll!' they shouted. When Banquo died at the hands of Macbeth's henchmen but his son Fleance escaped, the entire theatre groaned its sympathy and disappointment and someone leapt to his feet with the warning: 'It's a set-up, Mac. Watch those damned witches!' The role of the treacherous hags having been rumbled, this useful piece of advice punctuated the proceedings from then on.

Very early on, of course, Sam Mafekong felt that he should object to this unusual reading of the play, but he had his projector to mind and he took a long view, gambling on Macbeth's bloody and richly deserved nemesis to correct any distortions in his heathen audience. Alas, it was a gamble he lost. The appearance of Macduff, savage and unstoppable, crying for vengeance for the murder of his wife and children, caused an eruption of abuse. 'Stoolie!' 'Squealer!' and 'Boer pig!' were just some of

54

the insults directed at Macduff. And when he ran Macbeth through with his sword, a near riot broke out in the cinema and flying objects striking his precious screen forced Mafekong to stop the show.

It was a horrible blow. Sam found himself having to refuse requests for 'more culture' for exactly the same reasons as he had hoped to introduce some culture in the first place. The experience had embittered him. Yet a small flame of hope burnt softly in his heart. His faith insisted he remain optimistic. Certainly he remained enough of the missionary to find the proposition offered to him by the funny, skinny, dancing boy to be irresistible. Particularly since Lucky's offer of a film came with absolutely no strings attached. It was free. It had not been stolen (he checked on this) and Lucky's description of what it was about entranced the old man.

'It's about these swans which are birds with white feathers and huge arms. Who dance. Like this.' Lucky danced.

'I know swans,' Sam said. 'So it's a nature film.'

'And the Prince Siegfried goes hunting for these swans with his bow.'

'Terrific. So it's also got action.'

'And the Prince falls in love with the Swan, who is really a lovely girl who has been bewitched by a wizard. The Prince wishes to save her.'

Sam clapped his hands. A love story! A love story about dumb animals of which even the SPCA would approve! 'Do they marry?'

'They die.'

Sam was stricken. 'Oh no!'

Lucky softened the blow. 'Yet also they do not die. They pass by. And their friends the Swan Girls dance for them as they pass by.'

'Pass by?'

Lucky was unable to explain himself on this point. He waved his arms vaguely. 'They go somewhere at the back. Swimming away. You can see them, through the curtain – The Prince and the Swan Girl. Forever together.'

But this simply confused Sam still further. 'Go at the back? What does this mean? Go where?'

Lucky thought hard. Finally he came up with the answer. 'Overseas. And all the Swan Girls dance them goodbye. Like this.'

Lucky rose on his toes and spread his fingers in stiff fans which he   55 fluttered at his waist to suggest the skirts of the grieving swans.

'Don't do that, boy,' said the old projectionist. 'Only girls do that. It gives people the wrong idea. Okay, I'll show your film.'

And he sold out the theatre the night he screened Lucky's film. All his fellow Methodists came, for moral uplift. They also believed in being kind to dumb animals. Perhaps a few came because they wished to see exactly what a swan looked like. But principally they came because Sam assured them that it was a film about wild life and a story of the triumph of love over death, as well as being a musical extravaganza extremely popular overseas. The gangsters came too, in even greater numbers. They came because it was rumoured that Sam Mafekong had obtained a foreign film which was full of women who wore practically no clothes. Mr Ice declared that the women wore skirts so short they showed off their pants. Mantanzima offered as his opinion that some probably wore no pants at all. Two-Can Mafeti said that he had heard the film showed people making love to animals.

The first five minutes passed in stunned silence. The arrival of the Queen Mother was greeted with boos. The drunken old Tutor was loudly mocked. The presentation of a crossbow to the Prince was greeted with hopeful cheers. But it was the arrival of the Swans which did the real damage. A low rumble began in the rear of the hall where the heavy mob was sitting. The Methodists tried to contain it, clicking their tongues in annoyance and hissing at the gangsters to be quiet. But the rumble rose to a high-pitched electric hum as it became clear to the hoodlums that they had been duped. Then, in a body, like demented bees, they rose from their seats and flew for Sam Mafekong's projection room.

The old man, fearing for his equipment, tried to stop them. A blow to the temple dropped him in the doorway. He need not have bothered. They were very careful with the equipment, it was the film they wanted. They tore it from the projector, slashed it with razors, stamped on it, took a great grey cloud of it to the back door and set it ablaze. And when Lucky made his way from the dark cinema where the Methodists sat quaking in the blackness, they attempted to feed him to the flames as well and might have succeeded had the police not arrived in their van to investigate reports that foreign pornographic material was being screened at the Bantu Men's Social Centre.

The fact that Lucky owed his life to the hated cops did little to enhance his chances of survival in the township. It meant he did not dare show his face. It kept him on the outskirts, wandering the main road between the police station and the hospital, sleeping in the cannibalised hulk of a burnt-out Austin, supplied with food on secret visits by Granny Muriel. One night he ventured back to the cinema where in the dust around the back doors he found a fragment of his film. He sat in the car the following morning and held it up to the sun. It showed the entrance of the Magician's daughter, the Black Swan, Odile, disguised as the real Swan Girl; she was wicked, brilliant and shameless. The tall figure of Rothbart in his golden cloak loomed, leered and flung his spell on the Prince who clung to the false swan with swooning adoration, blind to the White Swan at the window who looked on like a grieving ghost at her own funeral.

Muriel watched over him, shaking with fear, convinced that it was only a matter of time before someone found the boy's hiding place. She foresaw another headstone in the bleak graveyard where Caleb, Rachel, Ruth and Sarah lay.

'What have you done to your granny? You are mad, stupid! Why must you make these people want to kill you?'

But Lucky scarcely heard her. He faced a problem, a puzzle. What he wanted to know was: how should he proceed? He felt sure Ilse had left some message for him and he waited for a sign.

The sign came unexpectedly.

On the road he passed the Doctor who devoured children. This time Lucky had no one to restrain him. He climbed on to the steel shelf that ran along the hoarding and found that the Doctor's face at this close range was pocked and dotted with stippled specks of colour. Red, orange, blue, these specks formed lines which ran away in every direction in orderly rows like the tips of the plants in a field of maize, or the stones he had once arranged in such strict patterns upon the graves of Granny Muriel's dead children. He found, too, that the lips of the Doctor, which at a distance appeared to wear a faint half smile of slightly sleepy benevolence, now seemed to be set in something very like a sneer. The pale blue eyes winked like swimming pools he had seen in the rich white houses of the big city. The Doctor's grey hair loomed cloudily. Lucky reached up as high as he could and tore at the paper. When he stepped down, the Doctor was blind. Where his eyes had been were two rough circles. Lucky felt satisfied. The only small thing troubling him as he glanced back across his shoulder was that his attack on the eyes had had the effect of enlarging and rounding them to a degree which gave the face a distinctly owlish cast. Lucky shivered. He hurried away.

Lucky sought out the General immediately he returned to the township. The journey had been painful and he had slept for some hours in the rusting Austin on the outskirts of the township which had been his home for nights past.

'You've been in the wars, kid?' the General demanded.

'To the ballet,' Lucky replied.

'That's rough dancing, boy,' said the General, looking at his swollen face and the blood congealed behind his right ear in a looping black crust.

'In the ballet, the Prince dies.'

'I'm sad to hear that,' said the General.

'And the Swan Girl, too.'

'That's bad.'

'But they're free at the end. They go sailing away, safe and sound, for ever and ever.'

'But dead,' the General reminded him.

Yet even as he said this he knew by looking at Lucky's face – so fierce despite the purple swelling that closed his left eye and the flaking ribbon of dried blood that ran from his ear up into the thick black curls – that the boy considered this to be an objection too light to bother with. In Lucky's eyes the fate suffered by the sad lovers seemed inconsequential beside the glory of their achievement, their defeat of the Wizard, and freedom. That was doubtless what the boy was seeing now, the dark angry eyes gleaming from the bruised sockets. Such eyes! The pupils were jet-black, the irises cloudy mauve, the whites traced with broken veins. The boy had probably taken several blows to the eyes. It was the force behind the gaze which was the most striking, the way the eyes stared through him – no, pushed him aside, thrust him out of the way.

He had the most curious sensation when the boy looked at him like that; it was as if he were an impediment in his field of vision, a rock or tree that hindered the boy's forward progress. Now the General was a determined and clever, ruthless, dedicated man. He knew varieties of danger and recognized them quickly. He understood when force was being brought into play. Such strength he measured in terms of police, guns, dogs, soldiers, trackers, helicopters. All these things he knew because they were the way by which he judged the seriousness of the force raised against him. But the boy's glance was something different, as powerful yet somehow more ruthless. This boy felt himself to be something extraordinary. He believed hugely in whatever he saw ahead of him, he knew himself to be unstoppable.

'Come with me,' the General said in his soft voice. 'I want to show you something.'

He took Lucky to the township lake. The surface rippled, the water lapped at its banks like a dark tongue licking its lips. The boy was glad all over again that there were no swans and no chance of their ever being seen on this sombre stretch of water. He was surprised by the number of people at the lakeside. Unexpected visitors. A couple of bus-stop loungers he recognized as Mr Ice and a vicious knifeman they called Candlewick because of the way his head tapered to a point which sported a single black tuft of hair. Such people were not too keen on the lakeside; it was so dirty and the mud was bound to ruin their expensive, highly polished shoes. And there was Moses Nhlunga, the owner of the funeral parlour. What were they all staring at?

The little crowd parted with a murmur when the people saw the General, though at the same time they contrived to suggest that they hadn't seen him at all.

Lying face up, one blue eye peering through a stiff curtain of blonde hair, Ilse wore a puzzling expression. There was something faintly comical in her look, in the way she both hid and peeped at him. She was wearing the same white bra and pants in which she had danced with him. Lucky bent closer to the cold white face. A little water ran out of her ear.

'The cops have been looking in the wrong places,' the General declared to no one in particular.

'She's been in the water maybe eight hours,' said the undertaker, with a professional glance.

'I saw her first,' said Candlewick. 'She was floating out by that old oil-drum. Only her head – it hit, hit, hit the drum.' Candlewick banged his tapering forehead with his fist to illustrate. 'Boom, boom!'

Lucky knelt down and took Ilse's hand. It was wet and heavy. He also felt heavy. Well, now she knew what the lake was for. There had been bodies on other occasions. His heart was sore. He pressed her hand and bowed his head. And yet, maybe there was something not too bad in this. He remembered the girl's extraordinary power. She had shown this in everything she touched. She knew what to do. Yes, there had been bodies before . . . but never a white one. Here was the sign he had been waiting for. He thought of the Doctor's torn eyes, shivered and drew away, all at the same time.

The General led him away. Behind them Candlewick picked up the Superman comic that lay half-buried in the mud and which Ilse had forbidden Lucky to touch, and he covered her face with it.

The General, glancing at Lucky, was astonished to see that his face wore a blazing smile.

'What's the matter?'

'She was clever! Oh yes. She came from Germany and she was clever! In the school, in the film, in the story, she always knows how to. Oh yes,' he repeated solemnly. 'Even now, she knows.'

'How to what?' The General was bewildered by this sudden jubilation.

'To fight.'

Lucky addressed these words to the distant features of the Doctor, whose torn blind eyes glared across the township. The General had to shake him.

'So what you want, boy?'

'To go to Germany.'

The General smiled. 'With no shoes?'

Lucky stood with one foot on the other. He spread the toes of his right foot and fitted them between the toes of his left, as if he also owned some wonderful puzzle to which he alone had the key. The General had read his mind.

'My Granny took them, to stop me dancing. But I do not need shoes to dance.'

'Sure you don't. But to go to Germany, you need shoes. Right?'

Lucky did not reply.

'And to fight, you need shoes too.'

The General addressed these words to a wretched, red-eyed, skinny, bare-footed, bruised and blood-stained boy. His smile was gone.

FIVE

The transport plane droned through the night. Its walls vibrated with the engines and its yellow cabin lights shivered on the faces of the young men sleeping on the hard seats. How strange that they should all be going to join the ballet! He had not thought that the whole country could contain so many people who thought as he did. The General had explained matters to him.

'You will get shoes. Tonight you leave the township. Nobody will see you go. In so many days,' he held up three fingers, 'you will be in Germany. There we have friends who will teach you all you want to know – many people who think like you. We are in 1965 and it is already late. Life is short and we have very little beauty. You like beauty. So do I. But we cannot eat beauty. We like dancing too, but we have nothing to dance for. Before we can dance we must be free. To be free we must fight. Let the day come when the present show ends and we will dance. All of us.'

'All of us!' Lucky echoed, his eyes shining.

'In the streets,' the General declared.

'On the stage,' Lucky continued.

'Centre stage if you like.' The General was slightly taken aback.

'And will no one hit us, or throw things?'

The General shook his head. 'Certainly not.' He pointed his forefinger in the air in front of him, so Lucky immediately recognized the shape of the pistol, cocked his thumb and fired an imaginary shot. Then he blew smoke from the barrel of the pistol. 'Goodbye, policeman,' said the General.

Lucky cocked his finger, pointed and fired. 'Goodbye, wizard.' He blew smoke from the barrel of the pistol. 'When I am in Germany, I will go straight to the people of the ballet. I will say my name and I will learn with them.'

The General nodded.

Lucky was content. He felt sure Ilse would have been pleased. He did not feel the bruises on his face. He did not care that his head hummed and throbbed when he spoke, or even when he blinked. Things were as they should be. The General was an interesting person. He had raised no objection to Lucky's plans. He was sensible. He did not interfere when a person decided to leave for distant places. In fact, he seemed to encourage it.

And so it was that Lucky sat in the big plane. They had reached the airport after two days' march through the bush and crossed the border at night. Now he was grinding through the sky with a number of other young men who slept, snored, groaned, shook themselves awake and slept again. Beneath them the African continent lay buried in cloud. Far below lay the Kalahari Desert, the Congo Basin and the Sahara, unknown and unseen as the plane shivered steadily northwards. Lucky smiled at his own reflection in the cabin window. How wonderful it was that unbeknown to him the country should be full of secret ballet lovers!

They landed in the early morning at a military airfield among needle-nosed jets and big-bellied transports. The mist was lifting as they came down the steps of the aircraft and were ushered into a yellow bus by men in dark grey uniforms who counted them, made energetic notes of their names and counted them again. In the first light, Lucky realised that most of the boys were older than him and bigger. The countryside through which they drove was a curious colour, dark green shot with wet grey. Even in the sunshine it looked wet. It was also somehow thick and pressed in, heavy, lush grass rode alongside the bus pressing closer than anything he had known at home. And the bus drove on the wrong side of the road.

They arrived in a small town. Lucky had seen nothing like it before. The buildings were short and squat, their walls painted many different colours: olive, mustard, rose-pink. Some of the roofs were pointed like churches. Perhaps they were churches? Others were shaped like onions, the walls were thick and there were many clocks, also in different colours. One big clock struck with deep brassy strokes that shivered in his ears. Then two figures appeared high up in the clock tower, a man in a long coat and a woman in a long dress who danced and bowed in time to a whirring tune which the clock played all by itself. How clever it was! He clapped his hands. Of course he saw that the figures were mechanical, their jerky iron movements told him that. But it was a pretty sight, the dancing couple in the sky. The clock stopped chiming and the figures vanished. Lucky's applause fluttered around the silent bus like a caged bird. How strange that his travelling companions should seem so unimpressed. They slumped in their seats. Some of them looked ill, others frightened, some lonely – a few even looked angry.

In the heavy traffic the bus slowed and for a moment Lucky thought it had come to a stop. In front of them was a big building, a hall of sorts with columns in the front and a handsome roof of red tiles and a group of pretty figures of angels and giants holding flowers high up in the 'V' where the sides of the roof met. Big wooden doors with metal decorations on either side, and large posters made Lucky's heart begin to thump. For in the posters the Swan Princess raised herself on her toes; the other leg reached out and up almost as high as her shoulder, her arms were lifted above her head tapering at the wrist into fingers stroking the air, making not one but two swans' necks. Lucky fell back into his seat, his heart expanding with happiness. Ilse had told him the truth. Here in his first town in Germany they were dancing *Swan Lake*. What a country! Everywhere the ballet ruled and ordinary people off the streets might approach those in charge with the simple request to dance, and would be accepted. White Germans or black Germans, this was the right place. He had arrived. He began to get to his feet. As he did so the bus, seizing a gap in the traffic, lurched forward and he was thrown back violently into his seat. When he looked again, they had left the town behind him.

'Wait!' Lucky implored.

But the driver ignored him. The other young men stared at him in alarm or amusement as the bus raced on. They were taken to a camp in a forest. There was clearly no dancing here. Instead there were grey overalls, leather boots, caps and large white men who spoke good

English in the same throaty accents as Ilse had used, the sound reminding him of chairs being moved across a concrete floor. He went straight over to the men and spoke to them as Ilse had taught him to do.

'My name is Lucky and I am here to dance. I wish to go to the ballet.'

'You must do nothing without orders,' they replied.

Chief among the men giving them orders was one named Captain Adler – thin, well-tanned, with a way of pointing his sharp nose at whomever he was addressing.

'Welcome to Camp Liberation,' said Adler.

They were taught marching and shooting. Lucky waited patiently for them to start teaching dancing, but nothing happened. He asked to leave the camp and go into town, but he was told firmly that trainees were not allowed in the town. Their presence in the country was a closely guarded secret and the town was out of bounds. All their needs were catered for in the camp. Each received a small sum weekly with which to buy soap, shaving requisites, cigarettes and sweets from the camp store. All this was provided by courtesy of the freedom-loving people of the German Democratic Republic, in solidarity with the legitimate aspirations of the masses of Southern Africa for independence, justice and peace.

They began by learning to march in formation. It did not go well for Lucky. He had enormous trouble keeping step, trod on the heel of the man in front and destroyed the entire marching order of the group. But their instructor, Captain Adler, was patient. Lucky was singled out and made to march around the perimeter of the parade ground, a small hunched figure in large black boots. He marched around the edge of the field several times while the instructor yelled in his ear, 'Left! Right! Left!' After a while he found the step. However, he could not understand that the arm is supposed to alternate with the opposite leg. Left arm, right leg. However often Adler started him that way, up came the left arm with the left leg and before long the platoon watching at ease of the far side of the parade ground rocked with laughter. Finally a compromise was reached, with Lucky marching fifteen metres behind the platoon, shoulders hunched about his ears, left arm and left leg in ungainly unison.

'And you are the man who wants to dance!' said Alder.

66   Shooting practice followed. The range was many kilometres away

and they ran there with full packs and rifles and arrived exhausted. Lucky's feet in the heavy boots were a mass of blisters and abrasions. In those days Adler's nose, already thin, grew more beaked and his lips tightened. He became what he probably always had been – an arrogant, sneering professional who told the recruits that he had toughened his muscles by testing them against nature herself and living rough, existing wherever possible on roots and grubs. He had eaten snakes, he said. He also explained that their rifles were so powerful that were he to stand six South African policemen one behind the other, a single shot would pass through all of their heads without difficulty. Several of the recruits were visibly impressed and shouted revolutionary slogans. Adler told them to shut up. Before they could shoot their policemen, they had to learn to aim carefully and he was going to train them to do that.

But first they were taught to move through the bush, 'like beasts'. Adler lay flat on his belly and pulled himself forward by his elbows. This was the leopard crawl. Lucky watched him twisting through the thick green German grass with his prominent, rock-hard bottom rising above the blades of grass and thought that he looked more like a fat snake than a leopard. When Lucky was forced into the leopard crawl, his elbows rubbed raw very quickly.

They then turned to shooting. They began firing over fifty metres at large circular targets coloured in blue, white and red circles. In front of these targets there ran a deep trench, in which crouched an observer who could mark hits on the targets by hoisting a circular metal disc on a long pole and indicating to the distant marksman his rate of progress. Lucky stretched out on the ground, squeezed the trigger and fired. His ears stung from the report of the rifle and the butt kicked him painfully in the shoulder. Behind him, to his enormous surprise, Adler – who was watching through binoculars – commended him. It seemed he had hit the target dead centre. In his excitement Lucky fired again. The man in the butts had no time to pull down his marker and took a bullet through the metal disc. A contraction of horror as he heard Adler swearing behind him made Lucky loose another round. This time he smashed through the wooden pole that held the metal disc. In a rage, Adler ordered him to make a leopard crawl to the 150 metre mark, and back.

Next, they used stubby black machine-guns, difficult to operate because you had to pull the trigger while at the same time squeezing the palm-release lever. If the action of the hand, palm and finger were not co-ordinated, the gun jammed.

'If your gun jams, on no account turn round,' Adler warned. 'Just put up your hand and I will come over to you.' He took up his position behind them.

They were firing over twenty-five metres this time. The targets were full-sized cut-outs of soldiers. All the soldiers had the same face, a fact which intrigued Lucky for the surprising thing was that this face bore a close resemblance to the General's. It seemed to him somehow wrong to be shooting at the General who had, after all, helped to get him to Germany. He wished the General were there now to explain to him why he was lying in this uncomfortable position firing bullets when, down the road no doubt, on the stage of the theatre in town, the wicked magician Rothbart was threatening to break the heart of the Swan Princess, Odette. His elbows were bleeding from his long leopard crawl and resting his weight on them was agony. He slowly squeezed the trigger. Nothing happened. He tried again. Beside him bullets spat and chuckled. He turned to his left: not much, just enough to catch the eye of Adler who was already walking towards him. The little gun snickered beneath his chin and Adler stopped dead. His face drained of colour, he swayed momentarily and for one horrible moment Lucky thought he had hit him. But Adler was unhurt. The bullets had flown past his face, which now grew dark and hateful.

'You stupid black baboon!' Adler yelled. 'You're under arrest.'

These words came back to Lucky a little while later back at the camp. When Adler spoke them to him on the shooting range he had been writhing in fear, confusion and dismay. But now, when he thought of the words, they gave him an odd glow of comfort. It was strange, but they made him feel quite homesick. Arrest had turned out to mean 'confined to barracks'. That in turn had meant the hospital, where they looked at Lucky as though he were very sick indeed, although he was actually feeling very much better. So much better in fact that later that night, when the lights went off and the trainees went to their early beds, Lucky crept from the hospital and slipped away into the darkness and walked into town.

He arrived at the theatre just as the Third Act was beginning. He bought a ticket and was allowed to take his seat at the moment when the Queen Mother arrived with the six princesses. Lucky clasped his legs to his chest, rested his chin on his knees and with heart pounding, watched the Prince spurn all six pretty princesses while his mother, the Queen, frowned and wagged her finger at her foolish son. Then there appeared at the door the fateful visitors. The Prince moved forward; he beamed. Lucky also moved forward in the darkness and muttered. Here was the evil owl wizard Rothbart and the girl by his side was not Odette, but his daughter, Odile, in disguise. Oh, how Lucky longed now for the guns he had used that day! Then he would show them. The Black Swan approached the Prince. Did the Prince not see it? But of course he did not. Now the real Swan Princess appeared in the Palace window, sadly peering at the Prince in the arms of the imposter. No one saw her, except Lucky. The evil magician triumphed, the Prince was bewitched, the spell worked, the Prince had broken his promise to the Swan Girl and he danced now with her wicked double . . . 'You stupid black baboon,' Lucky muttered in a choked voice. 'You're under arrest.'

But of course he knew it did no good. Some creatures you could not hold, no matter how tightly you locked them away or put them down or bound them up in chains or ropes. They escaped to do whatever they could, until time ran out. So he watched the story unfold and when the dead lovers sailed away into eternity, Lucky wept in the darkness and his tears left damp patches on the knees of his overall.

He waited for the audience to leave. There were surprisingly few of them. Perhaps people saw so much ballet here that they were used to it. Fortunate people! The ushers, who wore dark green tunics, went around the hall sweeping between the purple plush seats, and knocking them into an upright position with a rough blow of their broom handles. No one bothered with Lucky. A man in a black suit and a blue bow-tie wandered up and down in front of the stage, yawning and glancing at his watch. This man was clearly in charge here. He had a great round egg face, with fat pink cheeks that gleamed like light bulbs. From somewhere back-stage came the sound of laughter and doors slamming. The dancers must be getting ready to go home. Lucky slipped from his seat and made for the yawning man.

'My name is Lucky. I want to learn to dance.'

The manager examined the creature before him, who was speaking to him in a foreign language.

'Go home!' he instructed, 'We are closing the theatre.'

Lucky beamed at him. Clearly, the fat man had trouble understanding him. Unlike all the other Germans he had met, this one did not appear to speak English. Very well, he was not daunted. He lifted his hands; he would use the language of ballet. 'You wait here,' he waved this message to the manager. 'I will go there' – he pointed to the stage – 'and dance for you. I love to dance.' He crossed his hands over his heart.

Then he turned and leapt on to the stage with a reassuring backward glance and a smile at the manager and removed his boots. He rolled the legs of his overalls to the thighs, he rolled his sleeves to his elbows. 'I have come to join you. I love you,' Lucky signalled. And with that he began to dance, calling out the steps Ilse had shown him. 'Arabesque,' he announced. 'Pirouette' – his voice faltered.

The manager waved frantically at one of the ushers who was leaning on his broom watching the boy soaring through the air. 'Call the police,' said the manager. 'This man is a lunatic!'

'Jeté!' Lucky leaped imploringly from foot to foot.

They took him back to the army camp in the woods, making him crouch in the back of a car with a blanket thrown over his head. Lucky said nothing. At the camp he was locked in a cell. The following morning he was driven out to the same airport at which he had arrived only a few weeks earlier. A big plane sat heavily on the runway. Lucky was its only passenger. Adler accompanied him and made a short speech.

'You have satisfied your instructors that your course is now over,' he said. 'You have completed your training much sooner than expected. In the light of the special category into which you fall, it is felt by all responsible officials of Camp Liberation that it is unfair to deprive your comrades at home of your services. We wish you every success in the continuation of your struggle.'

When he had finished saying all this, Adler led Lucky up the steps into the aircraft. He looked at him and shook his head. 'You're a queer bird,' he said.

SIX

Lucky's enthusiastic reception at the camp in the bush was dependent upon several factors. He swelled the numbers of the fighting unit which lived in the heavily camouflaged tents, lean-tos and trenches. Then too, these guerrillas had never worked with a man who had trained abroad. His posting was considered an honour, a mark of esteem. The South African habit of reading into the lives of others what one hoped or expected to find there, ensured that his arrival was seen as a special sign of favour, of luck and of encouragement. To have completed several months of training in a matter of weeks, to have satisfied his German instructors that he was a combatant of rare quality, to have been overseas at all and to be so extraordinarily modest about his achievements – in fact to remain utterly silent – these were qualities which made those in the bush camp shake their heads with admiration. In that hot, dry, lonely place, pleasant surprises were few.

The camp was sadly depleted, no better than half-strength. It had once catered for upward of thirty men, Lucky was told by the Commander – a large-bellied, bearded man wearing a dark green beret and dark glasses, who was known simply as Comrade Joe. He shook Lucky's hand and clapped him on the shoulder. They were delighted to have a star performer, and they had lined up for him a very special mission which nobody else could undertake. The unit had transferred here after their base camp in a small town in the interior was bombed by enemy aircraft which had wounded a number of men. Not long after their decampment into the bush, the rains had come and the little river that cut through a stony gorge five kilometres away and which marked the border, was in brief, torrential spate and crossings into enemy-occupied territory were set back for several weeks. With the rains came dysentery and several more casualties. But at last missions were again under way and Lucky was congratulated for having arrived just in time for the major counter-offensive.

'Better out here fighting than back there being hit,' said Comrade Joe, jerking a thumb over his shoulder in a vaguely northward direction where, some fifty kilometres to their rear, their base camp lay. 'The jets hit us early one morning. Coming out of the sun. I happened to be outside at the time. They came in so low I could feel the draught. They hit one of our compounds and got several men. But their aim was way off target. They blasted the school, an agricultural college and a dairy. And they call that shooting! We certainly took some losses; but consider their score. They demolished a shed full of tractors and killed nine goats. And they seriously injured a couple of Congolese footballers who were staying in the compound next door. Of course, to hear them tell it, you'd think they had knocked out half our fighting force. Did they crow! It's all propaganda, you see. But I'm sure they taught you that at military college overseas.'

The fact that Lucky had been overseas was particularly impressive for Comrade Joe's second-in-command and logistics officer, a cheerful young man known as Uncle S. He had been a trombone player in a jazz band – so good he had thought of training in America. He amazed Lucky with a series of requests for news about European football teams, quizzing him particularly intently about a team called the Zurich Grasshoppers. Lucky shook his head. What about the Dynamo Kiev? Again Lucky shook his head and this time shrugged his shoulders. If anything, the esteem felt towards him by Uncle S. deepened still further. That a man should make a trip into what he called 'the magical ballplay of the superpros in the superleague' and yet not drink at the holy wells of world soccer, suggested to him a devotion to duty superhuman in its austerity.

'Didn't you even watch some games on TV?'

For the third time Lucky shook his head.

Uncle S. whistled. 'Awesome!' he said.

He carried with him a powerful Japanese radio tuned in to sports reports from the white broadcasting service which reached him with surprising clarity, bringing news of weekly fixtures played out in the townships many hundreds of miles to the south. Getting news on the big games in the townships was Uncle S.'s abiding obsession. To see him counting out grenades with his transistor radio pressed to his ear while an excited announcer reported that Swallows' centre-forward had equalled with a flying header in the fifty-second minute was to observe a man totally content with the world. The fact that the enemy did not play soccer, which was the most popular sport in the world, 'if not in the entire universe', simply went to show his extremely low rating upon the evolutionary scale. This was further borne out by the jet attack on their base camp. Here he strongly disagreed with Comrade Joe. The bombing raid on the Congolese footballers in the adjoining compound was not, in Uncle's opinion, a clumsy mistake, but a calculated assault by the rugby-worshipping enemy upon the favourite sport of freedom-loving peoples of the world.

The period when Lucky was in the camp was one of busy activity. Each morning small groups of men were armed by Uncle, briefed by Comrade Joe and went loping off into the bush, rifles held low, spare magazines dangling like holsters from their belts. This was the counter-offensive, Comrade Joe explained to Lucky. After the enemy attack on their camp, it was essential that a response be made.

'Offensive begets counter-offensive. We cannot allow the enemy to believe he has scored a win, or he makes propaganda. So we attack quickly.'

None of these raiding parties ever returned. By the end of the month Comrade Joe, Uncle S. and Lucky were the only men left in the camp.

This method was opposed by Uncle S. 'But what do we achieve? Where are the results?'

'We achieve effects. We get impact,' Comrade Joe answered him testily. 'Propaganda is more important than results. Sometimes I think you would have done better to have gone off like you wanted and played your trombone in America. You'd be better there than sitting here scorning the brave efforts of good men to free their country. What do you mean by talking about results?'

'This is 1965,' said Uncle. 'How long do you think we're going to have to keep on doing this before we win? How are we going to win without results?'

73

'The struggle goes on. But since you're asking, I'll tell you. Give it another ten years. This is just the beginning.'

'Why do we always have to be at the beginning?'

'Where's your faith?' Comrade Joe demanded. 'You've got to have faith. Rome wasn't built in a day. Lucky knows that. I'll bet you that's what they taught him overseas – isn't that so, Lucky?'

But Lucky did not respond. His silence was taken to indicate his thoughtfulness. It seemed to them to be a sign of a deep tactical intelligence which was no doubt examining the camp, its soldiers and officers, and measuring them against the immeasurably higher standard he had grown used to in the professional military establishment in which he had trained abroad. When he took to wandering about in the bush, this was put down to his desire to deepen his knowledge of veldcraft. It was also regarded as particularly wise, since the enemy had been making increasing use of Bushmen trackers who possessed uncanny powers of detection. These trackers could follow a target spoor day in and day out 'so damn needle-eyed they can tell if a ghost has passed that way wearing sneakers' was how Uncle S. expressed it. And Comrade Joe told him that Intelligence reported that the Bushmen trackers were put into collars like dogs and ran before the hunting troops on long leads.

It was an image Lucky found particularly unsettling. But still he said nothing. The truth was that Lucky was having trouble with his head. Something had gone wrong with it since his return from Germany. Perhaps it had gone wrong from the night when he had been arrested at the theatre. Again and again he went over the events of that disastrous night. Had he perhaps approached the wrong man? Had the man with the blue bow-tie been the caretaker and not the manager? Of course he realised now that they had not understood his language, but then he had shown them what he wanted, hadn't he? And why should the police have laughed at him? And why had they covered his head with a blanket? What was there about his face that they wished people not to see? What were they hiding? Or alternatively, why were they hiding him? He had been pained and angered by his experience. He had been spurned by the ballet, arrested by the police, locked up by the army. Something somewhere had gone terribly wrong and he wished to protest. He wanted to go back to that manager and demand an explanation. He could not understand it. On the one hand, everything he had been told had been true. He had come to Germany and there he had discovered the truth of Ilse's promise that in the outside world people were free to dance. Dance they did. But then why did they stop him doing so?

There was something worse. Since arriving back in Africa, he had made a discovery that frightened him. He could no longer fly. He went through the preparatory motions, opened his eyes wide and fixed them on a passing cloud, laced one set of toes into the other and waited for the rushing to begin in his ears, the sound he always heard before a take-off. He tensed . . . but then nothing happened. He remained earth-bound. Stuck. His feet were heavy. He hated his legs, he wished he could get rid of them. Worse still, he could no longer fix on destinations in advance. He remembered the places all right: the grey mist of England, the busby of the soldier outside Buckingham Palace. He could see the sidewalk where the lemonade sellers waited, with the skyline of Manhattan behind them. Doubtless they were waiting for him, for his blazing descent from the skies as in the old days. Perhaps they looked at each other and wondered aloud at his disappearance. 'Where is our friend Lucky?' they must be asking. He felt sorry for them and wished he could explain. But he had troubles enough. He went and sat under a thorn tree and shook his head from side to side, hoping that something would shake loose, that he would hear it rattle. The tree wore across its upper branches what looked at first like a thick hairy blanket, something which had been thrown there by a giant and snagged in the branches. It reminded him also of the thatched roof of a country hut, or of the straw hats worn by the Basuto fruit-sellers who used to hawk their produce in the township. After sitting under the tree for a while, he saw that it was in fact a gigantic nest for thousands of tiny birds who spent all day flying in and out with bits of grass in their mouths. When the birds all came together and roosted there, the whole tree shouted with their song. Lucky sat beneath the singing tree and hugged himself. He deeply admired the birds above his useless head. They built the singing city in the sky, they were as free as the air to come and go as they liked. Sometimes he stayed out all night under the tree and in the mornings he would watch other even tinier birds building nests that looked like old spiders' webs. He saw a very small bird, a little like a

75

dove, which shouted 'Hu! Hu!' at him from the grass. There were also running birds that made him laugh with their helmet heads rising to a peak, and cheeks that stuck out on either side of their heads when you saw them straight on. And their feathers were covered in tiny white dots which made them seem as if they were covered in white lace tablecloths. The thorn trees that dotted the veld between the camp and the river were full of birds which were decidedly less gentle than the tiny doves with their soft grey voices. These birds had white bellies and very sharp beaks and shouted, 'Go away! Go away!' so loudly and so often that he almost wished he could. One night he thought he heard lions roaring somewhere beyond the camp. But Comrade Joe surprised him by saying they were probably not lions, but male ostriches whose voices sounded very like lions. Lucky thrilled to know that a bird could be so powerful it might be mistaken for a lion. More than ever he longed with all his heart to belong to the family of birds. He was increasingly impatient to be off. To be elsewhere. Anywhere. He chafed with impatience for the special mission Comrade Joe had promised him.

Comrade Joe and Uncle S. became more and more depressed when all the soldiers had left the camp and none returned. They sat at the camp fire in the evening. Joe whittled a reed with a Swiss army knife. Uncle announced that his radio batteries were flat, which meant he would miss the big match on the following Saturday. They seemed to Lucky to be rather sad and yet also somehow slightly embarrassed. After a while he realised why this was so. When he had gone, they would be leaving. In fact, they were just as anxious as he was to be on their way. Comrade Joe confessed that he missed the whisky he had acquired a taste for back in their base. Uncle retorted that at the base you might get whisky, but you also got enemy raids.

'They can bomb me every morning, as long as I get a whisky come sundown,' replied Comrade Joe. He cut a notch in the reed and began to fashion a mouthpiece.

'Joe is merciless, it may surprise you to know,' Uncle S. said. 'I've known him execute deserters with his own hand . . . and sign the execution orders for traitors without flinching.'

'Our struggle is unstoppable,' said Comrade Joe. 'It will take more than jets and bombs to quench the fire in the hearts of our people.

Freedom!' He raised a fist in the air and the firelight danced on his knuckles.

'I reckon Swallows are going to murder Pirates on Saturday,' Uncle offered.

Comrade Joe fitted the reed to his lips and blew. 'Hu! Hu!' said the reed in a voice very like that of the little grey dove. 'We got today the shipment we've been waiting for, my boy.' He beamed at Lucky. 'Tomorrow morning you leave on your special mission.'

'A very important shipment. *One* important shipment is what you mean,' Uncle complained. 'What kind of supplier offers you a single sample of merchandise? What kind of friend is that? How are we supposed to fight a war with one of each?'

'Shut up with your supermarket talk,' Joe commanded. 'You damn Yank! We got all we need. This is a one-man mission.'

At first light the next morning, Lucky left the camp. He carried a compass, a map and in a pouch around his waist a heavy metal cylinder which bounced uncomfortably against his thigh as he walked.

'We will be waiting.' Comrade Joe said. 'Forward to freedom!'

Lucky did not believe him, for Uncle S. had already begun to strike camp. Joe's whisky and Uncle's radio batteries could no longer be denied. He knew they were just too polite to say so. And of course he was too polite to tell them that their map meant nothing to him. He left the camp some kilometres behind him before examining the scrap of paper. It showed lines, words, figures. He turned it this way and that, hoping that something would swim into focus, but nothing helped. Eventually he dug a small hole and buried it. He kept the compass because he liked the way the needle swung and quivered when he walked. And because it looked like a watch. He had always wanted a watch. He knew that the map was supposed to help him find out where he was going. But he did not wish to know where he was going. He did not mind that the others would not be waiting for him to get back, whatever they said. He did not intend going back. He was not really going anywhere. He picked up one foot and put it in front of the other and that kept him moving. His days for going places were gone . . . at least until he could clear his head of whatever blocked the space between his ears, kept him heavy and weighed down, stopped him taking off. He would have to do something. But he knew there was no going anywhere to do it; if it were done, it would have to be done here.

'Keep going, honey child,' he told himself in his Doctor Paul drawl. 'And you will find out what you have to do.'

These were the first words that he had spoken since the German police had covered his head with the blanket. He passed the singing tree. He waved. The angry sharp-beaked birds called, 'Go away!' Lucky shrugged. It was all very well for the birds to talk.

He came to the river. The rainwater that had made it run for a while had nearly gone and what was left moved sluggishly amongst the rocks. The banks were pocked with the hoof-marks of hundreds of animals. The mud was black and sticky. The round boulders were cold in the first rays of the sun as if they had just been born. He scrambled up the opposite bank and struck out into the harsh brown country ahead. Fifty metres away, a herd of buck lifted their heads and stared at him. But what was there to see? Just a boy carrying a bag walking through the veld. The buck lowered their heads with their sharp horns that pointed away in opposite directions and went on grazing. Having crossed the river he was home, except that he knew he was far from home. The buck were right to ignore him; he was a stranger here. Before him the veld stretched endless, vacant, indifferent. He found in a hollow depression a cache of huge eggs. He guessed at once what they were. Ostriches! Of the owners there was no sign. Gingerly he touched one of them. How heavy it was! How big and thick. He lifted it to his ear and shook it. Nothing. Though he felt the heavy liquid move inside, like a secret ocean. Gently he replaced the egg and went on his way. When he looked back, he saw a big bird swoop down to investigate the eggs. It pecked at them with its beak. Lucky smiled. Big as the bird was, it would not break those eggs. But then as he watched, something astonishing occurred. The bird hopped on one of the eggs and with a straining, heaving flap of its wings, very slowly took off with the egg clutched firmly in its talons. Now here was something! Lucky shaded his eyes as the bird rose higher, the egg hanging blackly beneath it. Then suddenly the egg was falling, turning as it fell. He heard it hit the ground and the bird dived for its meal. Lucky clapped his hands with pleasure at the bird's cleverness. Bombs! Was there no end to the brilliance of these native birds?

After that he went forward much more happily and as he went he sang the jingle from one of the toothpaste advertisements he had much enjoyed in what he now thought of as his past life, his life as a boy in the township:

> 'You'll wonder where the dullness went,
> When you brush your teeth with Pepsodent!'

Of course he knew that Ilse would not have approved. Not of the song, nor of his return to the radio voices. But he did not want to think of Ilse, nor of Germany, nor of swans. He wished only to be able to pick up one foot and put it down in front of the other and the song helped him with this, having a solid steady beat which enabled him to plant his feet regularly, even though this meant that the heavy cylinder in the bag around his waist banged painfully against his thigh muscle.

As the sun was setting, monstrous orange and violet in the blue-white sky, he came to the top of a small koppie from which he could see a road beneath him. In fact two roads, one leaving the other, making the shape of a catapult. He hurried down the stubbly slope, skidding on small stones and almost losing his balance in his hurry to get it over with. He was careful not to walk on the road itself, which was thickly covered with several inches of fine red sand. He remembered the story of the Bushman trackers running on their long leashes held by the white soldiers. He could see the little men with their red eyes and wrinkled yellow skins; he could hear their rasping breaths as they padded by on all fours. He made a wide semi-circle and approached the roads where they branched.

There was nothing to be seen. Everything was hot, empty and waiting on his next move. The country stretched to the metal horizon. Behind him the small koppie loomed. The veld opened its mouth, it yawned; it could swallow him if it chose. But it did not choose. Not for the moment. He decided on the left-hand track, about fifteen metres on from where the roads diverged. Down on his knees he scraped at the hot silky sand which reminded him of red cream. It also reminded him that he had not eaten for twelve hours. Into the hollow he laid the heavy cylinder. It was black and looked rather like the air filter on the old Austin car in which he had slept when the township hoods had hunted him, though it was not so rusty of course. He primed it as he had been

shown before covering it with sand, then he patted it for luck. He even sang softly to it: 'Go down little dawgie . . .' in his radio cowboy voice. When he stood up again there was no trace of what lay buried in the road, of the hidden egg he had planted. Then he felt so tired he could have lain down there and then and gone to sleep beside his buried secret.

Instead, he slept that night on the bare hillside overlooking the crossroads, curled among a jumble of rocks for protection and for the consolation their immovable bulk provided. Above him the heavens blazed like a field of flaming wheat or a diamond desert.

The next morning he set off, using his compass according to a method he invented. He simply followed the needle wherever it pointed. Perhaps the compass knew something he did not. By noon he was stumbling through exhausted water-holes where dried mud clung to the hard-baked sides of the depressions, cracked and peeling in a thick, ugly skin. His throat burnt and his head was more solid than ever. He did not know where to go next. In a fury he hurled away his compass and plodded on. Ahead of him were a few short dark, green trees standing out from the dry bush in the red sand. There were clumps of grass that swayed in the heat haze. He found a big rock and clambered on to it. He stood there waving his arms and shaking his head, sweat pouring down his face. He longed to jump off the rock to see if he could fly. Then a long way off he saw a black thing, like a huge head bouncing on the horizon. After a time he identified the thing as the top half of a jeep coming steadily towards him, shivering and shifting in the waves of heat, rising and sinking in the uneven terrain but always heading directly for him. He lowered his arms and waited. The jeep stopped in a slurry of pebbles a little way off and the men inside stood up and leaned guns on the windscreen.

'Police,' they said. 'Don't move or you're a dead duck.'

They put him in the back of the jeep. They did not mistreat him or hit him or abuse him or throw a blanket over his head, but their presence and his capture – these were enough to drive him deep into himself where he stormed and raged and hated. They had put him in leg-irons which were chained to the steel floor of the vehicle. They took out a map which he recognised as being exactly the same as the one he had been given back at the camp and had buried. How strange that they too should have a map!

81

'We have your maps. We have your friends. We have your guns. Now show us where you placed the mines.'

They searched him and found his scrap of film of *Swan Lake* and held it up to the sun. 'What's this?' they demanded. And before he could answer they threw it away into the wind. Lucky leapt despairingly after it. The chains rang on his leg-irons and he hung from the side of the jeep and the road blurred beneath him. They hauled him back.

'Show us the mines. We drive until you stop us. If we go, you go!'

Perhaps it was dangling head-first into space while the road raced beneath his nose that did it. But when they rammed him back into his seat, when he heard his chains rattle, his head seemed suddenly clearer. He stared at the backs of their necks which were thick, like bricks or trunks of trees. As he looked at the backs of their necks he found he could change them into whatever he wanted. The power was returning. He could make of these policemen whatever he liked! Still, he knew he could not fly. The chains and the leg-irons held him. But it gave him an idea.

The jeep sped on into the countryside. Then they picked up the road, the Y, the catapult where the roads branched, and the vehicle slowed to a crawl.

'Here we go,' said the policeman. 'It's up to you, boy. Find the egg you buried.'

Lucky hugged himself. He recalled the red, creamy sand at the crossroads, its warmth and its silkiness. He remembered too the ostrich eggs and the way the bird had tried to attack them and failed. Or seemed to fail, until it got its head right. That bird was clever. He saw again the long curve of the egg as it fell from the claws. The jeep stopped precisely at the point where the roads branched. The policemen looked at him, but they did not speak. There was no need. 'Left or right?' their eyes demanded. Lucky stared back. Eventually he smiled and gestured to the right.

'Get out and dig it up,' they ordered him. They unlocked one of the leg-irons and paid out the chain behind him as Lucky began to walk along the right-hand fork.

'We'll wait here,' they said and they began slowly backing the jeep up the left-hand fork.

Lucky kept grinning until it felt his face would split. The jeep inched backward. Then the sky burst open, Lucky took off on a flight which began in flames and ended in darkness and silence, and for some moments it rained policemen.

SEVEN

Perhaps Lucky's trial was full of music, though nobody heard it but himself. There were, for instance, the booming voices of the two men to his left and right who answered and echoed one another. There was the small old man at the big high desk to whom the man on his left and the man on his right raised their voices and whose own voice was a dry tinkle, like a cockroach scrabbling in a corner. Man on the left and man on the right shouted at each other; the words they used most frequently were bad and mad and sometimes the two words clashed in the air above Lucky's head and then the note deepened. At one stage the little old man at the high desk said that perhaps Lucky was both bad *and* mad and everyone laughed. Sitting on each side of the little old man at the desk were two more men who wrote continuously. Behind Lucky sat the audience, in long benches as if they were in church, and above them in the gallery more people who sometimes groaned in unison, a thunderous rumble. It was like the cinema show at the Bantu Men's Social Centre, except that this was no cinema show.

The three men who sat up at the big dark, shining desk looked to Lucky like some huge three-eyed truck. Their white faces gleamed like head-lamps. The intention of this truck, he knew, was to run him down. That was why the box with its four wooden sides in which he sat had been placed directly in the path of the juggernaut. The men to the left and right of Lucky waved papers at the three-eyed giant truck, hoping probably to distract its attention. But Lucky knew that sooner or later it would bear down on him.

Among the audience he saw several familiar faces. There was his

Granny Muriel and she was accompanied by the healer Marigold. Also among the crowd he saw several of the township hoods – Two-Can Mafeti was there and so was Mr Ice. In fact, numbers of young men were there and they seemed curiously excited. They were several times warned by the middle eye of the three-eyed truck that they would be expelled from the courtroom if their disturbances continued. Lucky searched in vain for the General. His absence was a particular disappointment because he had wished to explain to him that things in Germany were not all that they might be, and that many of the young men who set off to learn to dance might find themselves taken prisoner by extremely disagreeable people who threw blankets over their heads and abused them.

The big man on his left called for Lucky to be hanged. The man on his right asked for him to be put in a hospital. The three-eyed creature looked left and then it looked right, and it snorted.

Lucky was seated throughout the trial. In actual fact he would have much preferred to stand, because when he stood he did so with the help of two shining crutches which they had given him in the hospital. How he loved those crutches! He looked at them leaning against the wall of the square box in which he sat and his heart swelled. They were the most beautiful things he had ever owned. At night when he was alone he would run his fingers down their cool smooth strength, and kiss them. He had made swift progress on his crutches when he was in hospital. If truth be told, he could manage now with just one, but he never let anybody see that in case they took away the other one. He did not even very much regret the loss of his leg. One leg less seemed to release him from the ground, and he swung nimbly on his crutches like a trapeze artist.

His only really bad time had come on entering the wooden box for the first time when, to his great surprise, he had been placed in leg-irons. This disappointed and wearied him. He thought he had seen the last of those in the police jeep. He thought he had done enough to escape them. He even found himself beginning to grow angry, in the way that he had been angry in the back of the jeep. However, there were others in court who grew angry at this and after a while the leg-irons were removed.

'After all,' said the central figure of the menacing trio, 'a one-legged

85

man is hardly likely to run from the court!' There was appreciative laughter at this in which Lucky joined.

However, somebody was taking no chances for while Lucky was allowed to remain seated, the leg-irons with their clanking chain were transferred to his crutches. The crutches stood in the corner with the chains coiled around them like ugly, metal snakes. It pained Lucky to see his crutches taken into custody. Yet it also gave him a feeling of pride, for it showed how precious they were. It suggested to him that these people understood the things you might do with them. His head was clear now. He could do as he liked, he knew he could go where he pleased.

Lucky was asked whether he could follow the proceedings in English. He assured them that he could, and to prove it he half turned and nodded over the wooden wall of the box in which he sat at the audience massed behind him, and sang from his seated position: 'I love my little Toyota, and my little Toyota loves me.'

This was greeted with a burst of applause from the gallery and demands for an explanation from the three-eyed truck. The big man on Lucky's right explained that the accused had a gift for mimicry and had been much influenced by various radio programmes. The line quoted by the prisoner had in fact come from a radio advertisement.

But what, the cockroach voice demanded, was a Toyota?

A buzz of excitement tinged with bewilderment and a certain awe greeted this lofty, other-wordly question. It was explained for the benefit of the court that a Toyota was a Japanese motor car which was being imported into the country in increasing numbers. It had proved very popular. The Japanese were important trading partners and they enjoyed a special relationship with the government. The Japanese had accepted the designation 'honorary whites', thus allowing them to mingle freely with other European groups when they visited the country on trading missions, which they did frequently, enthusiastically and successfully. There followed several statements of support from all sides, commending this arrangement and reminding everyone that the country had much to be grateful for in the support of its trading partners.

The man on Lucky's left thanked the judge for these remarks, but
pointed out that there were several imports which he felt sure the

country could do without. These were the weapons of war, of terror, of destruction.

Everyone agreed with this and gave Lucky significant glances.

These glances were quite wasted for Lucky had gone away. He was back in the bush, in the back seat of the jeep as they approached the buried mine. The egg that lay warm and waiting in the sand. It seemed to him to have been the greatest thing he had ever done and its effects were all they had promised to be. His head had been cleared. The policemen had been removed. The blast had sent them flying. They had all been sent flying and he could remember the feeling of wind rushing past his face just before he pitched into the deep, dark pit. All had been as he wanted. True, there had been one small disappointment. Once having set off on this last flight, he had never expected to return. He had hoped to arrive in distant parts. Once he had taken off he had hoped to keep travelling – to arrive somewhere, anywhere, or nowhere. It didn't matter. But he did not expect to find, yet again, that he had been left behind. He had not expected to come to in the hospital. At least his leg had gone. He envied his leg which had gone on a decent journey. He imagined it traipsing through distant forests, across deserts. He saw it on the sidewalk in America conversing with the young sellers of lemonade. He saw it admiring the sights outside Buckingham Palace. Sometimes at night he awoke in his cell, because the stump where the missing leg had been hurt him terribly. Sometimes he dreamed that his leg had returned; he could feel it again and he would awake sweating and weeping only to find that it really had gone, and then he felt happy again.

A number of people spoke for Lucky. His Granny Muriel, speaking through her tears, declared that Lucky was 'mad in the head' but not 'bad'. The healer Marigold suggested that he had been possessed by a *tokoloshe*. There was some laughter in court at this and several of the rowdier elements, Two-Can Mafeti included, dangled from the gallery what Lucky recognised to his huge delight as a pair of ballet shoes. Lucky had feared that the hoodlums had been invited to this large room to pursue their vendetta against him, to finish off the business uncompleted after the abrupt end to his film show in the Bantu Men's Social Centre. But increasingly he came to realise that they exuded nothing other than strong, warm sympathy and even admiration. The doctor from Cologne confirmed that the prisoner was simple-minded, mentally backward. However, he was no lunatic. He had been corrupted by a naïve and seditious influence which had led him to imagine the world to be different from what it was. He had no record of violence, except for once having smashed a violin on loan to him.

Chairs scraped beneath the high bench facing Lucky. The engines were revving up. The man in the middle declared in his tinkling dry voice that he had come to the conclusion that Lucky was not mad but bad. Whatever his age was, he was old enough to know better. The case against Lucky, which was that he had caused the deaths of two members of the security forces, was proved. He asked Lucky if he had anything to say. Lucky's crutches were unchained and he rose slowly.

'I know that a small bird can break a big egg. An ostrich can speak with the voice of a lion. And one day we will all dance.' He allowed his crutches to fall to the floor, stretching out his arms for balance as he stood wobbling dangerously on his one leg.

There was a surge of excitement from the gallery and several more pairs of ballet shoes were defiantly displayed by their laces. The middle eye of the juggernaut now bearing down on Lucky took exception to this and warned rowdy elements in the public gallery that reports had been reaching him of disturbances in the township where, it was said, young men were to be seen dancing in the streets. Such behaviour could have only one result. Challenges to the forces of law and order would be punished, examples would be made and there was no sadder or more terrible example of this than the case before their eyes. He warned the young men who made a show of foreign symbols and exotic regalia with whatever subversive purpose, that they could expect no mercy and moreover, that these forms of foreign influence were unseemly, unmanly, unAfrican and – returning again to the example before the Court – extremely dangerous.

Then he sentenced Lucky to hang.

Only his Granny Muriel saw that Lucky had not heard the sentence, only she detected the warning signs that he was about to leave. She knew that he had missed most of his trial. Even though he could no longer lace one set of toes into the other, she could tell by his blind upward gaze that Lucky was preparing to take off. He had not altered